THE SCARECROW & GEORGE C

Mia Kerick

A NineStar Press Publication

Published by NineStar Press
P.O. Box 91792,
Albuquerque, New Mexico, 87199 USA.
www.ninestarpress.com

The Scarecrow & George C

Printed in the USA
First Edition
June, 2019

Print ISBN: 978-1-950412-94-5

Also available in eBook, ISBN: 978-1-950412-90-7

High school senior Van Liss is barely human. He thinks of himself as a scarecrow—ragged and unnerving, stuck and destined to spend his life cold and alone. If he ever had feelings, they were stomped out long ago by his selfish mother and her lecherous boyfriend. All he's been left with is bitter contempt, to which he clings.

With a rough exterior long used to keep the world at bay, Van spooks George Curaco, the handsome new fry cook at the diner where he works. But George C senses there is more to the untouchable Van and refuses to stop staring, fascinated by his eccentricity. When Van learns that George C is even more cold, alone, and frightened than himself, Van welcomes him to his empty home. And ends up finding his heart.

Their road to trust is rocky and, at times, even dangerous. And looming evil threatens to keep them apart forever.

Fair warning: You may want to strap in. It's going to be a bumpy ride.

For all who struggle to trust

Part One: Donovan

Do us both a favor:

check this out before you read

IF YOU'RE LOOKING to read a story about a sassy teenage gay boy who refuses to behave until he meets Mr. Wonderful in Senior Honors Physics, and then is dazzled into improved conduct and future monogamy, I highly doubt this is the book for you. Believe me when I say you should close the book right now—drop it into a recycling bin if you're all about keeping the earth green—and walk away. To this point, my life hasn't run according to a predictable romantic formula. I don't see a reason for this status to change.

Maybe you *think* you're into something darker, so an unconventional story will suit your offbeat mood. News flash, reader: loners spend significant time in bookstores. I'm aware of the kind of books that consider themselves dark, at least in a carnal sense, and many are categorized as "New Adult," just like this one. Between lewd front and back covers featuring tits, tats, and torsos, a threadbare plot is woven into a heavy fabric of inspired sex. You're not likely to find that shit in here, either—but don't I wish?

By now, you've probably noticed I possess a flair for the dramatic. Well, I look at it like this: creating drama staves off boredom. Not that I need to justify myself. But if you're still with me, you've earned a shred of my respect. So on second thought, maybe you *should* keep reading.

Stick along for the ride if it pops your cork...

Friday

I TOWEL MYSELF off after my second, extremely necessary, shower of the morning. Mom's cast-off pale pink towel is history thanks to unsightly smudges of black dye. *Whatever*. I did what I had to do, even if it was messy.

This morning, you see, I woke up and dyed my roots black. The urge to do it had been gathering steam for a few days—ever since the new kid started working at the diner. I picked up the dye on a rather compelling whim at the 24-hour pharmacy on the corner of Depot and Wilder Streets after work on Tuesday night. The rest is well-planned history.

I had to refer to a YouTube video so my roots would appear intentional, rather than a result of lazy grooming. And you may think I seem like a hot mess, but my crime against hair color has been done by careful design. Don't delude yourself—I wasn't going for the chic ombré look. Believe me, there's nothing trendy about me. I want bold black roots with zero transition to the rest of my white-blond hair.

I glance in the mirror over the bathroom sink and see the male reverse of Cruella DeVil. And I smile, having achieved the "what the fuck's up with his hair?" vibe I desire.

I suppose you want to know why I did it. That's an easy one, and I think you're going to appreciate my total candor. Drumroll, please: It's because even if I'm a loner, I'm not heartless. I'm different, and I flaunt it, which is my way of keeping it real with the world. FYI: "Different" is my PC way of letting the public know I'm strange, frightening, and maybe even slightly dangerous. So, it's better if that kid at the diner, and everybody else, looks away.

And you know what, boys and girls? I can help with that...

Here's how: I dress like a Halloween scarecrow. Yeah, yeah... You're wondering what, exactly, constitutes "scarecrow attire"? Go ahead, bookworm, google it. *I* did—I'm a visual sort of guy. You'll see images of rigid figures, some stuffed with hay, others skinny as the barn boards they're made of, clad in an unfortunate variety of secondhand clothing. I wear plaid flannel button-downs and overalls—yes, even to the wedding of a random second cousin last summer—peplum shirts of coarse fabric, and baggy, worn-out jeans, cinched at the waist by knotted burlap belts. Countless patches, Western bandanas, and an antique, oversized top hat finishes my retro cast-off style.

I laugh as I pull on today's hokey duds. I'm not what you'd call the picture of fashion. In fact, I'd wager guys rarely fantasize about their boyfriends sporting dirty, patched overalls and a hat like Abraham Lincoln's. But even if I take the hat off, you'll see my new jet-black roots—hard as hell to appreciate on a bleached blond. Dedicate the hair color upgrade to that guy at work who won't look away.

He probably considers himself eclectic and likes to think he appreciates life's more unusual things. Or maybe he's merely a Halloween maniac who is turned on by scarecrows with hair like straw. Incidentally, when I stripped my hair of color, I hoped it would further shock those around me into keeping their distance, but it seems to attract a certain fry cook.

I have fifteen minutes before I have to leave for the torture chamber most people refer to as high school, so I kneel in front of the coffee maker and brew a pot. I'll check over my take-home Euro History quiz while it brews. No, I'm not a nerd, but I want better options for the future than I've had in the past.

Before you ask, I have my reasons for wanting to appear shocking to the point of repellant. And for the most part, I've gotten my wish. Teachers and students at school, coworkers and customers at the diner, not to mention Mom and Jake downstairs, all glance at the floor when I walk by. But *this* guy fixes his gaze on me. Maybe my unnatural black roots will scare him off, the way a good scarecrow stuck in a vast cornfield scares away so many crows.

I just don't understand why he can't see how frightening I am.

You can see it, can't you?

*

"The freezer pop is here." Nobody laughs because it's not a joke—they all know it's true. I'm a damned cold human being, at home, at school, and here at my part-time job.

Yippee. He noticed I'm alive. And yeah, if you're wondering, I'm being sarcastic.

As I swish past Walter Ricker, I try to decide if it's worth the effort to flip him the bird for heckling me. By the time I reach my locker, I've decided not to acknowledge his rude remark with an equally rude gesture, mostly because he wants me to so friggin' badly. The dude craves attention—if not from me, then from his puny, not to mention captive, audience. I refuse to satisfy his narcissistic need. With a small yawn, I open my locker and toss in the oversized plaid flannel shirt I wear as a coat. I'm more careful when I store my antique top hat on the shelf. It's showing serious signs of wear and tear.

"Stand back everybody, unless you want freezer burn." More silence.

I reluctantly acknowledge Walter's persistence at inflicting his cruel humor on me. He's braver than the kids at school. Or maybe my disturbing reputation followed me from Leighton High School to Windsor Academy, but not to the Monty-Carlo Diner. Or, not yet. But nobody else in the break room moves a muscle. I have that general effect on people.

I step back so I can see my face in the mirror I superglued to the inside of my locker door on the very day I was hired last spring. Then I pull my bleached blond hair with newly black roots into a messy bun, but I'm distracted. At school, they cautiously call me Ice Queen, and I like it. At least, I prefer it to "freezer pop." It's more dignified.

"What's today's special, Rhonda?" I use my sharpest voice.

Rhonda Rosco is caught off guard, although she shouldn't be. The girl likes to think she's invisible when she leans against the wall in the corner by the window overlooking the parking lot. Immune to my wrath. But she's wrong—I see everything. And everyone. Don't get too comfortable, reader. I can see you too.

Rhonda smooths her khaki skirt over her full hips, tucks a strand of dull auburn hair behind her ear, and glances around to gauge reaction to the fact that today I chose her. She's not sure whether this makes her a target or one of the gang.

"What's the daily special, Rhonda?" I don't raise my voice. I never raise my voice anymore. I haven't shouted since I was twelve years old. Which is a different story for a different day. Don't hold your breath, bookworm.

"P-pot roast. With g-gravy and mashed potatoes. And mixed veggies…with garlic butter."

Want to know my secret to success in the realm of human intimidation? I choose my victims wisely. A different worker each day, so they can never relax. I rarely vary from my course, as routine calms me. Still peering in the mirror, I carefully apply the dark red lipstick I keep on my locker shelf. It has to be perfect to alarm them. And just like yesterday and the day before, I can literally *feel* the united stare of my bewildered audience of waiters and fry cooks as it descends upon me. I'm like a fatal accident on the side of the highway—a scarecrow boy sporting dark red lipstick and now, jet-black roots. They don't want to look at me, but they're compelled to. Face it; if *you* were in the break room, you'd be staring too.

"Thank you, Rhonda," I say, careful not to sound even remotely thankful, and sure in the knowledge I'll again become invisible when they get what they came for: a good long gawking session at the strangest person they know.

The lipstick I wear is as dark as red gets. I'm convinced it discourages customers, and everyone else, from entertaining the slightest urge to kiss me, or do anything else with my mouth. One of my two bosses, Monty, is a huge, silent, and—like me—intimidating guy. But surprisingly, he's cool with the whole "boy wearing makeup" thing. He won't let me wear black lipstick when I serve food in his diner though. Believe me, I tried it. It's a big *no can do*. I have to settle for sporting black lips at school.

I frequently consider getting a stitched-lip tattoo along the entire length of my mouth—above *and* below my lips. That'd certainly do the trick in discouraging oral fantasies—am I right, or am I right?

After hanging my messenger bag in the locker, slipping my feet out of my combat boots and into black sneakers, and tying a red apron around my waist, I walk back the way I came onto the floor of the Monty-Carlo Diner.

"You're on section *C* tonight, Donovan. And you've already got customers waiting on you at C25." Despite being young enough to be his son, Carlo is Monty's partner in all aspects of life. Where Monty does all of the employee scheduling, orders, and other behind-the-scenes types of work, Carlo is always present at the diner, sticking his nose into every other aspect of the business. Lurking over our shoulders by the cash register, hanging in the kitchen near the fry cooks, lingering in the hallway by the restrooms—his job is to make sure everything at the diner is correct, clean, and cooked to his standards. And I've always suspected Carlo was the man behind the "no black lipstick at work, Donovan" decision.

"Yes, sir." I'm always respectful to authority figures, with the exception of my mother and her boyfriend. Not sweet, by any means, but respectful. In this case, I know who butters my bread. I may be a scarecrow, but I'm no dummy.

I deliver glasses of ice water to an elderly couple I recognize from their frequent diner visits. The pair is memorable because they say in unison, "God bless you, dear," at the conclusion of every meal. And they're as familiar with the diner's menu as they likely are with Bible verses. The pair is ready to place their order before I have a chance to ask them what they want for dinner. As usual, they detail how they'd like their grilled cheese sandwiches cooked.

"Past golden-brown, dear—we find them tastiest when they're almost burned."

The weight of a gaze on my back presses like a flattened palm. And in my hair...like fingertips running through my new black roots.

Over the past eight years, I've grown adept at recognizing the almost-physical sensation of being watched. My lessons in this began at home when I was ten. By the age of eleven, I knew exactly when Jake was gawking at me—he lurked in the hallway when I was in the shower so he'd be in perfect position to watch me run down the hall to my bedroom, wrapped in only a bath towel. And he stared at my lips as I sucked up strands of buttered spaghetti at dinnertime; somehow, I was aware he was looking even when my gaze was fixed on my bowl. At twelve, I told Mom her boyfriend should take a picture instead of constantly staring at me, because it would last longer. She reported my accusation to Jake, who claimed I was a "lying little bitch."

I know what being studied feels like. But the gaze on me is soft and warm, not creepy and chilling, like Jake's. Or catty, like the staff's. Or scared shitless, like everybody at school. Somehow, I also know all of this.

When I turn around, I see him. The new short-order cook is staring at me from behind the lunch counter and sipping iced tea from a red-and-white striped straw. Shoulder-length curly brown hair—cut in the style of an eighties rocker—and expressive gray eyes with dark lashes that define them like eyeliner. Doesn't he know he's a vision of a bygone era? And he apparently hasn't got a clue—the way the rest of the staff at the Monty-Carlo Diner does—that Donovan Liss is a stone-cold loner. A danger to him at worst, and in the best case, a lying little bitch who has zero interest in learning so much as his first name. So I do what I do best; I tell him to go to hell without using words. I simply stare right back at him, as brazen as can be, and scratch my nose with my tall middle finger. When he glances away, I revel in my success until a surge of guilt floods me, because maybe it *was* a bit like kicking a puppy. But if scarecrow attire and black-rooted straw-like hair don't repel him, a nasty gesture surely will.

I don't let anybody in. Not even adorable shaggy rock 'n' roll puppy dogs with sad, dark eyes. Do me a favor, reader—hold off on the blame game until you know my reasons.

*

His name is George...well, George C, since there's already a George who works at the diner as a delivery person. Despite how much I didn't want it, this knowledge was forced upon me tonight.

"George C, I need a large fry!"

"George C, put extra mayo on the fish filet!"

"What's taking so freaking long on those cheeseburgers, George C?"

Everybody eventually learns the name of the short-order cooks. It's inevitable. And necessary, if you want your orders to be plated in a timely and accurate fashion. Which I do.

I'm usually pretty stressed-out by the end of my shift. Forcing a smile on my lips and a genial tone in my voice for an extended period of time is exhausting. The walking back and forth and the lifting of heavy trays don't faze me. But after six hours of being on my best human behavior, I'm more than ready to hurl one of the potted spider plants from the large tables by the window across the room into the breakfast bar. And watch it smash against the plaster. And slide to the floor in a pile of brown and green chunks.

The image makes me smile, as I head back to the break room. I rarely smile, so it catches Carlo's attention. "Are you grinning, Donovan?"

I fight the urge to tell him to go fuck himself. In order to do this, I picture a thick slab of brown bread smeared generously with butter. This job is my bread and butter. "Yes, sir. It was a good night for tips." I jingle the cash in my apron pocket.

"Well, you should smile more often. It works well on you. You'd probably take home even more tips."

"You're hotter when you smile, Van."

Shadows of Jake follow me everywhere. Through gritted teeth, I utter, "Thank you, sir."

"Enjoy your evening, son."

Carlo's now grinning, like he's going to ask me if I have any special plans for tonight, as it's a Friday, and isn't Friday night date night? Or is date night Saturday evening? I don't give a shit, but I shake my head deliberately in an effort to discourage him.

"Monty and I are going to listen to a band, down by the lake. It'll be chilly, but I'm taking along a couple of sleeping bags so we'll stay warm." His voice is dreamy, and I swear he has stars in his eyes.

At least I don't have to worry about my bosses wanting to get busy *with me.* They're too passionately busy with each other. *How fucking sweet.* "Sounds like a blast. Have fun."

This is about the extent of small talk I'm capable of. I hurry to my locker, where I pull out my messenger bag, lift the flap, and after untying my apron, I pour in the cash that's weighing me down. Then, I pull on my flannel coat and oversized top hat, change into my boots, sling my messenger bag over my shoulder, and head back through the restaurant to the front door.

I hate that I have to come and go through the restaurant. That I have to be the real me—not food server me—in a place where I have a well-defined role. Not a role I'm exactly comfortable with, but one I can deal with. And I can "fake nice" when I'm working, but beyond that, it's too much of an effort. And when I finally step onto the street and pull in a long-awaited breath of cool air that doesn't stink of greasy food, he's beside me.

"Hey, Donovan."

"Van," I say and sigh.

"I'm George...George Curaco."

"Whatever." I pull the flannel shirt around me tightly and turn away from him. But I have a job to do before I storm off. "You need to leave me the fuck alone, George C...or find a new job."

I wonder if he steps back or gasps or covers his mouth with his probably greasy hand in response to my rudeness, but there's no sound of movement.

"You can't stop me from looking at you. Or asking you if I can carry your bag...to wherever it is you're going tonight."

I grit my teeth—it's a trick I learned when I was a kid. To prevent me from screaming.

"Can I carry your bag?"

My jaw still clamped, I shake my head.

"*May* I carry your bag?"

"Leave me the fuck alone." Since I've voiced everything necessary on the subject of him and me, I brave a final glance. I need evidence that the puppy is down on the sidewalk, writhing in pain, having been kicked by the lying little bitch. But he doesn't appear even slightly pathetic. The kid is studying me—his eyes seem serious, even sad, as usual, but he's wearing a smirk. It hits me that George C isn't sad at all. "It's just your eyes... they look sad, but they're not."

"Just like your words. They make you seem mean...but *you're* not."

Oh, yes, I am!

George C pulls my bag from my shoulder by the long strap. "So where are we going?"

I snatch it back with a hiss. It's louder than I intended. "I have no clue where *you* are going, but *I* am going home. Alone." George C has succeeded in getting under my weathered, burlap scarecrow skin. This surprises me, as it hasn't happened in years. I don't curse at him again or spit on his shoes, which I've been known to do. I just storm down Depot Street in the direction of our duplex. To the second-floor suite I claim as mine. The Batcave. My safe space.

"I enjoyed our chat, Van. Really, I did." His voice is soft and raspy, yet it carries all the way to me, and I'm at least ten steps away already.

It must be the direction of the wind.

Saturday

THE FBI PAID me a visit when I was fifteen years old.

Okay, okay...I know what you're thinking. And maybe I *am* exaggerating. I can't swear on a stack of Bibles that those men in black suits were from an *actual* federal agency, but what does it matter? This is my story—yeah, they're *my* thoughts I'm spilling to you so generously. I can exaggerate if I want to.

I rise from the couch, where I slept last night. And the night before. All right, maybe I sleep here a lot. Every single damned night. I'm just not comfortable in bedrooms, not that I owe anyone an explanation. As I make a pot of coffee on the upside down plastic bin between the microwave and mini fridge, I recall an insane Saturday morning in the fall of sophomore year, a morning a lot like this one, when *some* form of law enforcement—two men in plain clothes who flashed a badge—dropped by our house in Leighton to check up on me. They summoned my mother, and we all sat stiffly in the living room, debating as to whether or not I was a danger to myself and others.

As it turns out, a group of Leighton High School parents had reported me as a potential school-shooter type of personality. They'd actually called the police on me, told them a combination of truth and lies—that I was totally antisocial and had threatened other kids with fictional guns I have no access to, nor interest in. According to the officer perched on the loveseat in our living room, a "surprisingly large number of individuals have informed us that you, Mr. Liss, are highly antisocial and unreasonably angry, and threaten violence regularly." They'd further reported that, although I was respectful to teachers and staff, the adults at school weren't comfortable with me either. In short, I was "consistently sullen and intimidating." My very presence disturbed students and staff alike.

I can't blame any of them for their fears...it's a vicious and nonsensical world we live in where a young adult male, for the most part, is apt to do anything. In many places, disturbed people my age *can* buy a gun and use it to wreak havoc on others at school, in theaters, in churches. I totally get how people are afraid of it happening to them—you probably are too—but the thing is, I don't want to hurt anyone. I just want everybody to stay away from me. Because maybe...just maybe, *I'm* afraid of *them*. Of everybody—students and staff. Of my family. Of the random disturbed teenager who gets his hands on a gun. Of the entire world.

My fear is bigger than yours *and* theirs—maybe even put together.

I'm not asking for your pity; I'm pretty sure I wouldn't get it if I asked. I'm not exactly the empathy-inducing sort. But the truth is, nobody protected me when I needed it—in my very own home where I should have felt safe. Acting "consistently sullen and intimidating" is my way of taking care of myself. I am sullen and intimidating at home...at school...at work. I'm sullen and intimidating 24/7, like it's my job. And it's exhausting, but it would be far more exhausting to let my guard down.

By the parental accusations that sprang from their children's fear—accurate on the sullen behavior, but inaccurate on the weapons accusations—I knew I'd successfully separated myself from the rest of the world, which *had* been my goal. Even so, somewhere deep within the glory of my success, I felt depressed. On that Saturday morning in October of sophomore year, sitting on my couch and smirking at the cops as I was questioned, lectured, and then sternly warned, I was disheartened. Nobody worried over the boy who was in such despair he'd alienated himself from the world. Everybody worried about their own asses, their kids' asses. This is the kind of world we live in, I guess.

True disclosure: Nobody—not my guidance counselor or my mother, for a start—has even once reached out in an effort to determine the how and why of my antisocial behavior. But I'm better at hiding the fact I give a shit about stuff like that now. And I'm better at flying low under the radar at Windsor Academy than I was at Leighton High School.

Anyhow, after assuring the cops I wasn't planning to shoot up the school—not to mention Mom and her live-in boyfriend, Jake, didn't even own a gun I could steal to do it—they reluctantly departed. I was certain, as they closed the front door, that those men would keep a future eye on me. As soon as they drove away, Mom beat me with Jake's belt for putting our "family" on the radar.

His belt wasn't burlap. I couldn't move for two days. And those men didn't return to my house to find out where the bruises on my face and body came from. So if they actually *were* keeping an eye on me, it wasn't a particularly attentive one. But I'd achieved my short-term goal: no one from Leighton High School wanted to be near me, let alone in a bedroom with me, which was what I feared most. I was safe. Except for when I was at home.

Things are different now because Mom and Jake have grown kind of scared of me too.

The second floor of our new house is like a complete and compact apartment in itself, which is convenient. I never have to go downstairs to make food or take a piss; in fact, days at a time can pass me by without seeing Mom and Jake. I have a living area where I keep a microwave, a mini-fridge, and a coffee maker. I've got a bedroom and a bathroom all to myself. I have no idea how I survived in the tiny ranch in Leighton with my less-than-loving mother and her perverted boyfriend for so many years. All we share now is a main entrance. And if I time it right, our comings and goings consistently miss one another.

I take my mug of coffee back to the couch. Not one for television—a good thing because I don't own one—I lift my sketch pad off the coffee table. If my former schoolmates and their parents caught a glimpse of the dark, disturbing daily entries in my current sketch pad, they'd call Homeland Security, for sure. *Just sayin'.*

I'm a talented artist, but only when it comes to drawing monsters. For some reason, the creatures that haunt my mind are the only things I can make real on paper. In such vivid detail, they almost look alive. And by committing them to paper, I'm able to expel them from my brain. Well, for the most part—as long as I stay out of bedrooms.

Shit had gotten so out of hand at Leighton High School we had to relocate. And I had lofty goals for a fresh start when we first moved to Windsor last year. Hopes I could achieve "normal human being" status—that I could stop dressing like it was Halloween and start drawing hearts and rainbows in my sketch pad, like gay boys are supposed to do. And sleep in a damn bedroom instead of on a living room couch. And maybe even talk to kids at my new school. But the damage was too deep. By this, I'm referring to the scars left by so much fear.

My revised goal is simple survival. The good news is I'm still *here*, drinking coffee on the couch. "So far, so good" is how I see it.

I grab my pencil and start to sketch. I hardly have to think about what I'm doing. As it moves, my hand seems to have a mind and a purpose all its own. I don't even have to think as I draw. Ever had that kind of thing happen? It's warped and wonderful at the same time.

I watch and wait for the monster to appear. And like I said, it's as if the hand working is not my own. Will today's monster be the disturbing rendition of Beauty's Beast, minus every last one of his endearing characteristics? Or will it resemble a dragon, but with a forked tongue and daggers in place of teeth? Maybe my hand will craft the familiar image of an obese male body with a fire-eyed skull balancing on his shoulders where

Jake's head should be. Or perhaps I'll fashion a new creature, born of the paradox from which I suffer—my paralyzing fear of human interaction and my simultaneous devastating need for it. A contradiction within me I've admitted to no one...except now, to you.

So keep it under *your* oversized top hat, my dear reader. Got it?

As I draw, I slip into a familiar daze. I float to the tiny crawl space in my head that holds all the reasons for why I am the way I am.

It's pitch black in here, and very cold. I crouch in the corner with my arms hugging bony knees to my chest, a last-ditch effort to hide since the walls are smooth rock and offer no nooks for me to slip inside. Although it's too dark to see a hand in front of my face, I squeeze my eyes shut. Just as I did when I was younger.

When the monster comes, I can't see his face or body. Thanks to the darkness, not to mention my sealed-shut eyes, his identity is masked. I tell myself I wouldn't recognize him if he passed me on the street, or in a dream—even though I would.

There's no doubt when the monster is looming above me; I recognize his closeness—I recognize him—by the way he smells. Spicy, like sweat and nachos. And by the way he touches me. By the mass of his paw fastened to my shoulder. By his heated breath, whooshing in disturbingly steady intervals on the back of my neck. By strength born of sheer bulk, allowing him to flip me gracelessly onto my belly as if I'm a child's doll and bearing down upon me with his enormous weight.

I grit my teeth as I strain against his overwhelming heaviness. As I voice my refusal, I think of Mom, and then block her from my brain. She can't help me. Or she won't.

When it's all too much to take, I change forms. I grow cold and hard, a chunk of rock on a mountain in winter. And slippery, as I'm fully ice-glazed, I slide from his grip and press my rock-body into the smooth granite wall. He can't find me now. Frustrated by my lack of response, he stops...

I'm frozen in place, just more ice-cold granite in the wall. And I wait.

The monster growls and then murmurs that it'll be okay, and to give him a pretty smile, but I don't. He tells me my mother won't believe me, and he's right. He brags that he can make me do what he wants, and he's right again. After a while, when I'm sure I can be hard and cold and still no more, he grows bored with the game and leaves without another word.

Like always, I want to follow him out the door—at a safe distance, of course. I want to go somewhere I can be warm and safe. Most times, I do this, knowing he's gone and won't return to my bed tonight. But now—for the first time ever—I'm frozen to the wall. I hid too well and have become part of the rock. Maybe I'm safe, but I'm so cold...I'm way too cold.

I want to move, but I can't—except for my hand. The one I draw with. It's free and can't stop moving. Sketching. Or am I waving, in the hope I will flag down someone...anyone...who can help me?

A new gaze falls upon me, warm and gentle, but as heavy as a down quilt. Someone is finally here to help, even if no one was ever there before.

I startle myself when I fall out of my trance. From a dark and frigid crawlspace deep in the earth, I'm dropped into a sunny autumn Saturday morning on my plain, light brown, fake suede living room couch. With my coffee cup beside me, still warm and full, and my sketch pad on my lap. And George C's face staring up at me in black and white…

I drew George C, the new short-order cook from the Monty-Carlo Diner.

Is he my newest monster? Or is he the one who pulled me from the wall?

*

Work is slow for a Saturday night. Slow, as in, it's completely empty in here. Windsor is a good-sized city, and the Monty-Carlo Diner is well priced with decent food, so I'm not sure why nobody's here. Maybe the crowd will arrive late. Late-night diners are lousy tippers, but such is the life of a student/waiter. The other servers are huddled with George C at the bar, talking up a storm, getting to know him. Every once in a while, a wild burst of laughter assaults my ears—I can't get any peace. When I'm at work I want to be working, goddammit. I want to be able to slip into my "fake nice" personality and earn tips.

"Come on over and hang out with us, Van," Walter calls in a teasing voice. "You seem so pitifully lonely."

"I'd rather chew on glass," I reply. Since I never raise my voice, he probably didn't hear me.

The head waitress, Nikki Nelson, is what the cooks call "hotness personified." A twenty-something-year-old woman who enjoys being sexy and plays it up to the max. Who isn't so afraid of being noticed that she has to dress like a scarecrow to frighten the world away. And maybe I'm jealous of her freedom; sometimes I wish I could be pretty rather than so aggressively strange. For some reason, though, she doesn't avoid me like the plague *or* want to break my spirit like the others do. "Leave Van alone. Can't you see he wants no part of you, Ricker?"

"Yeah, you're right. Donovan Liss has got *so many* better things to do with his time."

Funny. I'm sitting in a corner booth alone, studying my short-clipped glittery black fingernails, stressing out about the lack of customers, because I'm at work and there's no work. And no work for a waiter means no tips. So yeah, my dance card is chock-full.

"How about I give you something to do, Walter? It'll keep you busy until the crowd arrives." Nikki glances around and nods. "Time to fill the ketchup bottles. And Rhonda, you can help him."

They drag themselves off their bar stools and start to collect ketchups, leaving George C all alone. Walter shoots me a dirty look. I scratch my nose with my middle finger.

It's time for the staring marathon to begin, I predict when George C lifts his eyes and our gazes crash. I dread it more than usual because of how his face appeared so unexpectedly on my sketch pad this morning. An uninvited guest in my tiny apartment, for sure. I glance at him again, if only to prove my prediction, but I was wrong. His attention is caught by a couple of guys who enter the restaurant.

George C stares at them for a few seconds before he stands and scrambles toward the kitchen. But he's too slow. The two burly dudes grab him by the arms and drag him toward the door.

"Hey! Where are you taking my fry cook?" Carlo literally runs across the restaurant and plants himself in front of the door. I'm surprised at his speed. He's a short man, slightly pudgy, and his leather loafers aren't made for running. He skids to an awkward stop.

"We gotta chat with Curaco for a second, that's all," the larger of the two very large men replies.

"Well, George C is working tonight, I'm afraid. So he can't talk with you gentlemen right now." Carlo's chest is puffed up like a male bird in a courtship display.

"Hey, take a look around, little man," the smaller guy barks. "It's dead as a doornail in here."

"George C has takeout orders to fill. So if you young men aren't planning to sit down and eat dinner, it's time for you to leave."

I'm impressed. Carlo never seemed like the *Braveheart* type before. I'll probably end up sketching a picture of him tomorrow morning since saviors have apparently become my new artistic subject.

"Billy has a message for you, Curaco. And we're supposed to deliver it," the smaller huge dude says to George C in gravelly voice.

The more massive guy leans down. "We'll talk to him later about it, Jonah."

I glance at George C. He's as white as a sheet, and his eyes are wide and panic-stricken.

"We know where you live, Georgie," Jonah says.

"Uh-huh." George C's raspy voice cracks.

"You're such a fuckin' wuss!" Not-Jonah bellows, as if booming volume makes an insult more potent.

By now, you've probably guessed—I'm not much of a fighter. I'm not even close, at least, not in the physical sense. All I do to battle the world is use passive-aggressive responses to stay in control. I dish out sarcasm like I was born to do it. But something, don't ask me what, has me rising from the booth and strutting to where the two big assholes and George C wait by the door. "You're still here, so you kids must be hungry."

I spit out the words, and then I grin in their faces; they glare.

"I'm pleased to inform you that today's special is Bacon-Cheddar Macaroni and Cheese."

"What the hell are you going on about?" the one named Jonah asks me.

"Children—and in particular cranky toddlers—practically inhale it. I think you kids won't be able to shove enough of the stuff into your dirty pie holes." I offer menus, but they slap them away. The menus hit the floor, just like George C's chin before he grabs my arm.

"They aren't eating here, Van. They're leaving." He looks at me, but it's not his usual lazy, sizing-me-up kind of stare. It's much more urgent. Maybe it's even a warning. "I'll talk to you guys later," he tells them. He's still gawking at me.

"You sure as shit will."

As soon as the men leave, Carlo says, "George C, I'm going to need to talk to you in the break room."

Why do I give a damn what goes down in the break room? In fact, I hate it that I care, but I'm afraid Carlo's going to fire George C for bringing trouble into the diner. Before the late-night crowd arrives, though, the kid's back behind the bar, flipping burgers.

I breathe a sigh of relief and then curse myself out.

*

Other than Carlo, I'm the last one to leave the diner. It's Saturday night, so Rhonda and Walter have places to go, and George C slipped out when I wasn't paying attention. Not that I would have said anything to him, but I hope his "conversation" with the two assholes doesn't end up killing him. Because they seemed as mad as hell when they left.

Carlo finds me in the break room. "Thanks for staying late tonight, Donovan."

"You're welcome, sir."

"You can call me Carlo. Everybody else does."

I just nod, hoping to avoid a sappy conversation I don't want or need. Plus, I like calling him sir just fine. Respectful—strictly to authority figures—and impersonal. Just like me.

"Next Saturday night, I'm going to need two more servers and an extra fry cook, especially if it gets as busy as tonight did."

"Smart." I suck at small talk. As if you hadn't noticed.

"Okay, well, be careful getting home."

"I always am." He's offered me rides home a hundred times before. I've never once accepted, so now he knows better. I grab my messenger bag, dump my tips in, and change shoes. Then, on goes the plaid flannel coat and the top hat. Carlo takes my apron from my hands and walks me to the door.

"Goodnight, son."

I shrug and head out the door. I take a few steps so Carlo thinks I'm gone, and then stop to take a much-awaited cleansing breath—my first inhalation of cool, nongreasy outdoor air. But I'm disturbed by a high-pitched wheezing sound.

"Is somebody there?" The noise is coming from a small alleyway between the two buildings. I think it's an injured animal...maybe a cat. I step in the direction of the sound. And it stops. "Is somebody there?" I ask again.

No answer. I turn around to leave, but then there's sniffling. Coughing. Moaning. These are human sounds. Despite the fact that my gut is screaming not to do it, I turn back and head into the dark alley between the buildings. The crawl space in my head is all around me, and I'm almost too scared to move, but I keep going. There's a shadowy figure on the ground pressed against the foundation.

"Are you all right?" I ask. This person is *not* experiencing a high point in his life.

"I'm okay." It's a raspy voice I recognize. I'm not scared anymore.

"What happened to you, George C?" I crouch slightly so I can better hear him.

"I had a...little talk with...a couple of guys."

"It didn't go as well as you hoped?" I ask.

"No...it went exactly as I expected." He coughs a few times.

"You should come out of this alley. I mean, don't you think it's time to go home?"

George C releases a humming sound that makes me think he's considering my suggestion. Then he says, "I can't do that. They know where I've been staying and might go there looking to dish out some more."

"So you're just going to stay *here*?"

He's quiet for a few seconds. Then he says softly, "Uh, it's my plan at the moment."

A million thoughts rush into my mind, all at once:

He can't sleep in this alley—it's cold and dirty here.
How badly is he hurt? Does he need to see a doctor?
Do I give a shit? And if so, why do I give a shit?
I don't like people, but this doesn't mean I enjoy human suffering.
I should help him.
I should invite him to come home with me. He'd be safe there.

I don't know him—he could hurt me.

But you don't have to be a stranger to have bad intentions. (Lesson learned courtesy of Jake and Mom.)

"Come to my place." The Batcave. My safe space.

"You don't want me there."

He's right; I don't. "One night. You can stay for one night. Until you sort things out."

George C coughs. And then he moans. "I...offered to walk you home last night. You told me to leave you the fuck alone, remember?"

"Maybe you're right, but so what? Today's a different day." I reach out to him, and he takes my hands. He grunts as he stands. I grunt when he doesn't let go of my hands. But I don't pull away. "Can you even walk?"

"Yeah, no problem." With that, I pull my hands away and head for the street. He follows behind me.

When we reach Depot Street, George C's injuries are evident. Or, at least, some of them are. His sad eyes are swollen. His thin lips aren't thin anymore. His eighties hair is stuck to his head. "You're a mess."

"Thanks."

I turn in the direction of my apartment. He turns more haltingly and with greater effort. I'm not confident he's going to make it all the way to the Batcave. "Come on."

As we walk, I question my sanity. I change my mind about letting him come over, and then I change it back. I worry Mom or Jake might see him going up the stairs and think I'm getting soft—that I actually have a friend. Or a lover, God forbid. I think and rethink these things over and over. It's rather torturous, to be honest. But it's clear this guy's in pain. I'm pretty sure I can protect myself from him, considering his weakened condition, if worse comes to worst, which it has in my life before.

"I live up there." I point to my second-floor apartment.

"Stairs? Shit."

"I'll help you." I unlock the outside door as quietly as I can and push it open. From our shared entryway, the blaring of Mom and Jake's living room television can't be missed. "Come on," I whisper.

It takes two full minutes to climb a single flight of stairs with him leaning heavily on me for balance. I almost lose my hat three times. Opening the door at the top of the stairs is one of the hardest things I've ever done. And it's not because the door is jammed or George C is leaning on me, but because I haven't voluntarily let anyone into my life for years. I grit my teeth.

"Home sweet home," I say as we check out the mostly vacant space. He'll never know I think of this as the Batcave. That's a secret. I'm sure he has plenty of his own.

"It's nice."

I don't thank him. First of all, it *isn't* nice. It's plain and basic—completely undecorated and needs a paint job—but provides a roof over my head where I can be mercifully separate from my nasty mother and her loser boyfriend, who I sincerely believe would rather sleep with *me* than her. Second, I don't give a single shit what he thinks of the Batcave. "You want to wash up? The bathroom's over there." I point to the door closest to the microwave.

"Yeah. I should probably clean these cuts." He dabs at his bottom lip with his little finger.

"Well, go ahead. I'm gonna change my clothes." George C will be shocked to see my sweats aren't scarecrow-esque.

We go our separate ways. I pull on gray sweats and a plain white T-shirt. Then I sit on the couch and wait for him. It hits me that I'm gritting my teeth, but I simply can't stop.

"Van..." The bathroom door cracks open a few inches. "I hate to ask...but do you have any extra sweatpants and maybe a T-shirt I can borrow? My clothes...are too bloody to put back on."

I gasp. And for the record, I *never* gasp. I'm way too cool. But just then, I did. *His clothes are too bloody? Well, shit!* I nod in response, even as I realize he can't see me. "I'll find you something to wear."

In the bottom drawer of my bureau are what I think of as "comfy clothes." And reader, this is another little detail I'd prefer you keep under your hat. I search through for something that will fit him. I've never studied George C's body; it's not my style to do something so creepy. But from what I recall, he's a fairly slim guy. I'm skinny too, more so than him, but my baggiest pair of sweatpants should fit him. As a result of a laundry error, they're pink, but he won't care—they're clean. Every last one of my T-shirts are white and loose fitting, so I grab one and head back to the bathroom. The door is still cracked. "Uh, George C. I got you some clothes."

His hand shoots out of the opening. "I appreciate it a lot." He doesn't insist I call him George, and I wonder why.

Again, I nod, plant my ass on the couch, and wait for God knows what. *This is not me. This cannot be me. I've never had a guest here. I've never even wanted to have a guest in the Batcave.* It's too late to change my mind, though. Maybe I'll sleep with a butter knife from my silverware bin underneath a couch cushion.

When he emerges from the bathroom, I can't stifle a smirk. George C wears my white V-neck T-shirt. It's quite snug on him, and my pink sweatpants cling to what many people would consider to be all the right places. People who are not Donovan Liss, the human freezer pop, according to our coworker, Walter. I'm surprised at how fit George C is. I've never noticed the shape of his body, mainly because I wasn't looking and I don't give a shit, but also because he wears baggy camo pants and oversized black T-shirts to work.

My smile fades when he lifts his arms to hang his used towel over the edge of the bathroom door. The T-shirt drifts up and exposes the damage those assholes did to his back. It's mottled with deep purple bruises. In some places, his skin is broken and raw. I wonder how much of his body is covered with marks. "They kicked you?"

"Uh-huh. A couple times." He grits his teeth when he sits on the other end of the couch, and I realize I'm no longer gritting mine. "You look nice," he adds.

I look nice? In sweatpants? Maybe he's not such a huge fan of scarecrows, after all. "Want something to drink?" I ask. It's all I can think of to say.

"Water, please," he replies. "You don't have any Advil, do you?"

I go to the bathroom and pour water from the tap into two clear plastic cups I keep on the back of the toilet. Then I snatch the bottle of Advil from the medicine cabinet and balance it between them. As I walk back, I nearly drop everything with shock when it hits me that I'm not scared.

I'm. Not. Scared.

FYI, I'm freaking *always* scared.

"Here." I hand him a cup and the Advil. "What happened to you?" I can't believe what I'm doing. I'm asking a question. I'm getting involved.

What surprises me further is I'm able to watch as the window to George C's soul slams shut. He blinks once, and when he opens his eyes, for all intents and purposes, the guy is gone. I recognize what's happening because it's what I do best. I close myself off to everyone. And right now, George C is just like me. "Jonah and Mayo, the guys you met earlier tonight at the diner, asked me a question. They didn't like my answer. And...they let me know how unhappy they were."

It's too late when I realize my mouth is hanging open. I'm actually waiting for more.

"That's really all I want to say about it. 'Kay?" He glances past me to the far wall. Since nothing hangs there, it's obvious he's just trying to avoid my eyes.

I nod because right now, *he is me*. We're exactly the same. Looks like I'm not going to need to sleep with a butter knife tonight.

"You don't have a TV?" he asks, probably hoping to discourage further discussion with mindless sitcoms.

"No. If I want to see a movie or a rerun of a TV show, I watch it on my computer."

"I'm saving up for a laptop."

What? Every kid I know has a computer. Why doesn't George C have a damned laptop? I don't ask. But I do ask something else. "You're new to the diner. What were you doing before that?"

My houseguest yawns and stretches as widely as his bruised muscles allow. "I was busy selling my old laptop—needed the cash." He winks and then yawns again. "I'm beat."

"Literally or figuratively?" I ask with a smirk. Sarcastic humor eases awkwardness, right?

When he tilts his head, I realize I've totally lost him. "Am I sleeping on the couch tonight?" he asks.

This conversation is a done deal, I can see. He's exhausted and sore from a hard day of work and having the stuffing beaten out of him. And what's more, he has no plans to share the details of what happened to him today. It's none of my business anyway. I'm better off not knowing. Because, God knows, it would kill me to care. "No, you can sleep in the bedroom."

"With you?" *Now* I have his full attention. His puffy eyes crack open a bit wider.

"In your dreams, George C."

He smiles, and a drop of blood oozes from the split in his lip. "I wouldn't have been able to enjoy it anyway... I'm a hurting unit."

I wait for the prickles of fear. The fury. The sense of helplessness... *I'm alone in a room with a man who is thinking about fucking me.* I wait to be caught up in a wave of agitation, but the ocean is calm.

"That's a lie. I'd still enjoy it. You're...like, an intriguing dude."

"I..." I have no idea what to say. I've been called a lying little bitch. A freezer pop. The Ice Queen. A potential school shooter. And other insults I've worked damned hard to earn. I even call *myself* a creepy scarecrow. But "intriguing"? This is a first. "I'm exhausted too. You take the bed. I'll be fine here on the couch."

"I can't kick you out of your bed."

"It's not a problem. Believe me." He doesn't know it yet, but I never lie.

"Well, thanks." George C stands and takes a few steps toward the bedroom. Then he stops and glances over his shoulder, right at me, in the sizing-me-up way I've come to expect. "You saved my butt tonight."

This is another first for me. And again, I'm caught without a snarky comeback, so I say, "Go to bed."

Sunday

HE HASN'T EVEN woken up, and I want him gone. What was I thinking when I invited him here? I'm a stone-cold loner and I like it that way. I worked long and hard to alienate every last person I know. George C is a risk to the solitary life I've created. The very narrow, and very safe, pathway in which I exist.

It's nearly ten by the time he emerges from my bedroom. For the past several hours, thoughts have been churning in my brain, twisting up tightly and wrapping around one another. I'm not okay with sharing my life, not that the guy who slept in my bed has any interest in sharing anything at all. And my stress instantly increases when I notice what's in his hand.

George C is clutching my fucking sketch pad. "You drew a picture of me?" he asks.

"Where did you get that?" I hiss.

I notice the smug grin on his swollen lips. Even his puffy, puppy dog eyes have a smile in them. "It was on top of your bureau. Imagine my shock when I saw *me* looking up at me when I walked by."

I still have no explanation for why I sketched his face in my trance. No clue whatsoever. All I can think of to do is toss out an accusation. "You were snooping through my shit."

"Come on, Van. You're doing me a huge favor here. Why would I betray your trust by snooping?"

I shake my head. "Well, the favor is done." I stalk up to him and snatch the sketch pad. "You can leave now."

George C nods like he's seeing the big picture here. "I'm sorry I embarrassed you. I shouldn't have said anything. I guess I just hoped the sketch meant you've been thinking about me like I've been thinking about you."

"Well, I haven't. Did you take a peek at the other pictures in the book, you goddamned snoop? They're all of monsters. And your face is there because you're a monster too...always staring at me, like you do at the diner."

He glances at the coffee maker. "I suppose this means you're not going to make me a cup of coffee."

"Get out, George C."

"Can I borrow your clothes? I promise I'll bring them to work nice and clean."

"You can keep the fucking clothes, for all I care."

George C goes into the bathroom and grabs the pile of bloody stuff he left on the floor. He sticks his feet into his sneakers and shuffles to the door. "Thanks for everything. You have a great bed."

I wouldn't know. I've never slept in it. *"Good-bye."* I'm careful not to raise my voice.

Monday

MAYBE I'M THE Ice Queen—cold and detached—but let me tell you, I've got suffering eyes. And I hate them for giving so much away.

I stare into the fake glass mirror in the boys' room by the auditorium. My haunted gaze is like a window to the pain and sorrow and fear inside me. And the weakness—but the kids at school have no clue about this small detail. So even when it's what they want more than unlimited cash, beer, and no more unsightly zits on their chins, my fellow students at Windsor Academy hold back on tormenting me because since they don't understand me, they're afraid of me.

By design, it hurts for them to look at me—my tortured eyes, my scarecrow clothes, my unnatural jet-black lips, my coarse hair. Believe me when I tell you, *nobody's* gaze lingers on Donovan Liss—except George C's, but he's not here at school. Students wrinkle their noses and squint their eyes when they're forced to address me, and they always keep our interactions brief. Only I know the truth: they've succumbed to a well-laid plan for my complete isolation. And even when they desperately want to go there—to tease and humiliate me without a hint of mercy—they don't. Like I said, deep inside, they're afraid of yours truly. They've heard false rumors about the school-shooter thing from Leighton High School. Their parents surely remind them I *could* be dangerous, so they should always be civil. "Don't cross that Liss boy—he's not stable."

I drag my fingers beneath each of my eyes, smearing the eyeliner to accentuate my existing dark circles. I trace my mouth with a new tube of black lipstick. Then I stare into the warped stainless steel and admire the character I've created. The evil scarecrow-clown no one here at school dares to laugh at. I turn and walk toward the door. Eddie Riley, the burly captain of the Windsor Academy hockey team, steps aside to let skinny ol' me pass by.

Nobody—students, teachers, nor custodial staff— gives me the time of day as I journey to my locker, exchange my messenger bag for my Euro History notebook, and continue on my way to class. I'm invisible, again by design, until Mr. Sweeney greets me with a quick nod, which I return. I sit with my WWII project partner, Veronica Cherry, who was selected at random by Sweeney's fickle finger of fate technique in which he closes his eyes and lets his finger choose our partners. To her credit, she didn't groan when she plunked her ass in the desk beside mine.

"Hi, Van. Did you finish your part of the Holocaust report?" When it comes to academics, she will go where no student has gone before. She's actually willing to talk to me.

I analyze her narrowed eyes and then notice her nose isn't yet wrinkled with disdain. I'm sure I can fix that. "What if I didn't?"

She shrugs, and her gaze drops to my notebook.

"Are you gonna kick my ass? I mean, I could sink your Euro grade." I make a toilet-flushing gesture with a coordinating whooshing sound.

Veronica sighs. "Did you do it or not?"

I pull the printed description of the Auschwitz concentration camp and a sketch of Rudolf Höss out of my notebook and slam them onto the desk. "I do my work, Cherry."

She stares at the sketch. "Oh, my God, this is really good."

I huff loudly as if I don't care about the compliment, but I do. "I draw monsters like a pro," I mutter.

"You should do an illustration for the school literary magazine, Van."

"For Portals Literary Magazine?" I release a short spurt of laughter and end it with a smirk. And then I laugh again, but louder. A few kids from the aisle beside us turn to gawk, even though they've been warned by Mommy and Daddy not to engage me.

"Yeah. I'm on the content selection committee. I'd pick your sketch for sure."

I grit my teeth against the spark of excitement because she likes my work. I grit even tighter to resist the hope it engenders. "Like I give a shit about a ridiculous literary magazine."

"Well, maybe you *should* care, Ice Queen. We don't have a decent illustrator." Veronica pulls her part of the report out of a folder in her binder and places it underneath mine. "Think about it, okay?"

"Like that's gonna happen before hell freezes over." No matter how tightly I clamp my teeth together, I can't drive the new hope away.

*

George C is alone in the break room, lounging on the oversized couch when I arrive about fifteen minutes before my shift. I have no idea where Monty and Carlo found a lavender leather couch, but they did, and it's the centerpiece of the break room. In front of it is a hand-painted antique traveler's chest with a sheet of glass placed over its shabby-chic top so we can put our drinks down without leaving a water ring on what was so artistically destroyed a hundred years ago. Standard gray metal lockers occupy the wall behind the couch, and on the opposing wall, a bulletin board hangs covered in any news the workers want to show off.

In the center of the bulletin board is the front page of the *River Gazette* featuring a record time in the backstroke at a recent swim meet by the one-and-only Walter Ricker. Somebody drew a heart around his face in red sharpie marker. Beside it is a five by seven of Rhonda Rosco's senior picture. It's a pretty decent photo of her, not that I'd ever tell her this. There are a few cartoons scribbled on lined notebook paper of notable Monty-Carlo Diner customers eating their favorite meals. A sketch of the elderly couple that consistently blesses us after their evening meal is sketched stuffing their faces with burnt grill cheese sandwiches. It's kind of mean-spirited; I should enjoy the sentiment, but I don't. And a printed listing of a GoFundMe page in support of a teenager I don't know from Adam who is raising money to get Invisalign braces.

After dropping my messenger bag, coat, and hat in my locker, changing into my sneakers, and tying a clean apron from the laundry basket on the floor around my waist, it's time to choose my victim. Today, though, my victim selection is limited, as only George C and I are in the break room.

"George C, tell me about today's special," I demand.

"What do you want it to be?" His words come out a bit garbled. I don't mean to, but I glance at him. He's studying me in an annoyingly familiar manner. And his bottom lip is still as swollen as it was early Sunday morning.

"Jeez, George C—don't you think it's time to see a doctor about your lip?"

He shrugs. "How do you know I haven't?" He chuckles to himself. "And I'm kind of flattered. I think you care."

Nobody teases me or jokes or laughs with me. It's just not done. "If you're not going to tell me today's special I'll have to ask the head cook."

I start for the door, frustrated for more reasons than I care to explain, but George C bounces off the couch and is right in front of me before I can blink. "It's tortilla soup with homemade cornbread. I had it for dinner a few minutes ago and it rocked."

"Thanks." Shit, I sound appreciative. I'm seriously off my game.

"I'm the one who needs to thank *you*."

"For what?" I ask although I already know. He wants to thank me for giving him shelter on Saturday night.

George C grabs my wrist and pulls me toward the couch. For some reason, I let him. "Sit with me a minute."

Again, I acquiesce.

"Thanks for drawing the picture of me. You made me seem strong and brave and...well, you also gave me hope that maybe you think about me sometimes."

"That's ridiculous." I don't sound even slightly convincing.

"You can't stop me from believing what I want to believe."

He's right. "I guess I can't."

"Let me buy you a soda tonight at Wendy's after work. You know, to say thanks for putting me up at your place and making me the subject of your art."

This is the second time today I've felt a spark of hope I don't want. This time, it's in the realm of human connection; hope for this is surely dangerous. I grit my teeth, but it won't go away. "I don't know yet. I'll have to see if I'm thirsty at the end of my shift." *Why didn't I tell him to eat shit and die?*

George C smiles widely. His teeth are white and straight beneath his swollen lips. "Sounds reasonable."

I roll my eyes, which is more of an automatic response than something I choose to do. "It's almost five o'clock. I need to get out there." I nod in the direction of the restaurant.

"Me too. Come on."

*

As it turns out, I'm absolutely parched at the end of my shift. We're both standing in front of our lockers in the break room, and I'm just about to inform George C that it's his lucky day, when Nikki swoops in, grabs his elbows, and turns him around to face her.

"Hey, you know you're always welcome to stay at my place, right?" she asks, loud enough so everybody in the break room can hear.

"I sense a but coming..." he replies in a low voice.

She lowers her volume to match his. "Well, yeah...the thing is, my boyfriend is sleeping over tonight, and since it's a studio, you know, and we want some privacy..."

"No worries, Nikki. I'll find someplace else to stay."

"I hate to do this to you, kid. I'm so sorry." I steal a quick glance at her, and she appears genuinely regretful.

"It's nothing to worry about, Nikki. You've done way too much for me already." He leans into a hug she gladly gives. "You got me this job...and I've slept on your couch too many times to count. You're an angel."

"Okay. Are you sure you can find a place to stay?"

"I told you no worries."

Nikki pulls George C's head down and kisses his cheek. "See you tomorrow night." She rushes out to enjoy a night alone with her boyfriend.

I wasn't supposed to hear the exchange, so I act like I didn't and lean down to change into my boots. George C rushes off to the men's room, and when he comes back two minutes later, I smell soap. His exotic cheekbones (that make him more suitable as a model for Gillette razors than for frying burgers in the back end of a diner) have been scrubbed pink.

All of the other servers and cooks have gone home, so I don't have to tell him to keep it down when he asks, "Are you up for grabbing a soda with me?"

"I suppose it can't hurt," I reply, holding my head stiffly forward. This is uncharted territory—you know, the whole social interaction arena—and I'm not too proud to tell you I'm way the hell out of my league here. Not that you can help me.

George C stuffs his work shoes and the clothes he wore while working into what seems to be a jam-packed locker. Then he slides a backpack off the top shelf. "Cool."

I like how he doesn't make a big deal about this like he did over the sketch I drew of him. TBH, drama I don't create freaks me out. I throw on my coat, pull out my bag and sling it over my shoulder, stick my hat on my head, and step to his locker. "What the hell do you keep in there?" I ask. He can barely close his locker door.

"Would you believe it if I said everything I own?" Before I have a chance to ask him what he's talking about, he laughs too loudly. "Let's get out of here."

As we walk through the restaurant together, Carlo catches a glimpse of us. "You two together...uh-huh... that's really sweet, kids."

I never blush. In fact, I've mastered full temperature control of my entire facial region. To gain this level of control, I regularly practice keeping my cool. I run the most disturbing moments in my life through my mind, just to see if I can merely shrug, and, at most, roll my eyes, in response. But I never blush, as it's a dead giveaway of heated emotions, and as far as the world knows, I don't experience any emotions at all. Other than contempt. Yet, my cheeks start to burn as Carlo winks and nods at us. If he suggests we not do anything he and Monty wouldn't, I swear I'll kick him in the balls.

"We're getting a damn drink," I toss out with quiet but deadly hostility. It shuts him up.

I speedwalk the rest of the way across the restaurant, and George C even has trouble catching up with me on the Depot Street sidewalk. Once he's beside me, he asks, "Is Wendy's good for a soda?"

"It's fine." *This isn't a date*, I tell myself again and again...and again. *I'm just thirsty, and George C owes me.*

Once we're seated in a booth at Wendy's with our sodas on the table between us and my big hat on the seat beside me, I grit my teeth to help stay in control. Because, God knows, he's going to expect me to talk to him.

It's what two people do when they're having late-night drinks together, right? Am I right? I'm serious, reader—*I need an answer!* After people make small talk, the conversation morphs into more personal topics, doesn't it? *Doesn't it?*

I'm so screwed. Remember, I'm stone-cold...a complete loner. What the fuck have I gotten myself into?

"How come your folks let you have an apartment all your own on the second floor?"

George C is talking to me, and since I agreed to come here with him, I owe him an answer. "We don't get along. It's their way of kicking me out without actually kicking me out."

"Do you eat dinner with them...or maybe, Sunday morning breakfast?"

I shake my head. "We stay out of each other's way."

"You don't sound heartbroken over it."

"That's because I'm not. Not at all. It works better this way." Well, I responded like a human being, and I'm still alive. It wasn't so bad. "Where do you live?" This is a calculated question, based on the conversation I overheard between Nikki and him in the break room.

"I'm kind of between places." He grins. And winks. I sense distraction.

"Where do you go to school?"

His grin widens. "I'm actually not in school anymore."

Okay, maybe I *am* distracted. But I must have done something right to make him smile. Even it's with swollen lips. I know his game because until I met him, I played the distraction game better than anybody. I just go about it differently—I use intimidation to sidetrack people. "How old are you?"

"You're full of questions tonight, dude."

"Isn't it why we're here together tonight? To talk?"

He's surprised at how direct I am. Frankly, I'm surprised too. But hell, I'm curious.

"Look, Van, my life is a little bit crazy right now, and I'm just trying to make ends meet. I'm not gonna go into details, but I'm also not gonna lie to you. If you aren't cool with that, I get it, and I'll walk you home, and what's done is done."

Apparently, his ends are not meeting. "I'm cool with mystery," I assure him. Like keeping my distance from Mom and Jake, it's better this way.

"Good. I'll tell you this much—I'm not with my family anymore. I took off last summer right after high school graduation. Since then, I've been doing a little of this and a little of that. And right now, things are upside down for me."

"I hear you." Something about George C makes me want to talk to him. To tell him things I shouldn't. "We moved to our place on Depot Street last year because if I didn't have someplace separate from my family, I was going to do the very same thing as what you did." Until now, we've been staring into our sodas, but when I say this, we both lift our eyes from the table and our gazes collide. "Plus, I was having some trouble at school."

FYI, reader; I am entirely aware this is a major understatement.

"You and me, we're sort of the same," he says.

I'm not the kind of person to grab at human connection, but I think he may be right. I nod and it's enough.

For twenty minutes, we shoot the shit. He, ironically, loves '80s rock. I'm not much into music; it makes me melancholy. Raspy voices set to haunting melodies allow me to think of things I'd rather forget. I'm almost too embarrassed to admit it, but since he fessed up to his Bon Jovi crush, I do. I tell him I'm obsessed with the TV show, *Friends*, which I realize is also ironic, seeing as I don't have any. I've watched every episode of it on Hulu. George C's a dog person. I'd prefer a ferret if I was willing to share my life with an animal. He likes ferrets, too. His favorite food? Pad Thai. Mine? Pad Thai. And the next time we hang out, we're going to go to a Thai restaurant.

So maybe tonight's not-really-a-date isn't a one-hit wonder. I'm not sure how I feel about this, so do me a favor and don't ask.

"It's a school night for you, isn't it?" he asks me when I yawn.

"Yeah. But this is more fun than sleep." I can't believe what I just said. And then I ask another question. "Where are you going to sleep tonight?"

He sucks the bottom of his soda dry. "You heard what Nikki said to me?"

"I didn't mean to eavesdrop. I just heard."

"Well, I know some people. I'll figure out a place to stay."

"You can't go back to where you were staying before, wherever that was, because those two thugs know where you live. Right?"

"Sort of."

"You're basically homeless."

"Basically. But I'm decent under pressure, and I'll figure it out."

"Stay with me." We're both surprised at my invitation. He shakes his head, but for some godforsaken reason, I persist. "George C, I don't even sleep in my bedroom—don't ask me why. It just sits there empty."

"I didn't invite you here to get something from you."

"I know that. And you should be aware that I never lie. If I didn't want you to stay, I wouldn't have asked." George C lowers his head into his hands, so I continue. "If it makes you feel better, the bedroom is all I'm offering you. I buy my own food and heat it in the microwave—you'll have to do the same for yourself. I clean up after myself. If the bathroom gets slimy, I'll send you in there with a toothbrush. This is not a free ride at all."

"You for real, Van?" he asks.

"Why the hell not?" I counter.

"But you're in school...I can't be there when you're not."

"It's my apartment. Nobody goes up there but me. Believe me, Mom and her loser boyfriend have no interest in sharing sweet family moments with yours truly. I can even lock the door at the top of the stairs if it makes you feel better."

"I...I think that'd work. Yeah, I'll stay with you."

"Great. Then let's get our butts back there because I've got to wake up in five hours."

We throw away our cups and walk the half mile to the Batcave.

Tuesday

IT'S BIZARRE TO wake up to the smell of coffee brewing. I'll admit my first response is to shoot upright on the couch, clutch my fuzzy Hello Kitty blanket to my chest, and search around frantically for the sort of thief that brews coffee before robbing someone blind. When I remember I have a houseguest—one I invited here of my own free will—an enormous black cloud drifts across my living room and settles directly over my head. Is this a symptom of depression? Or is it simple fear?

Before I have a chance to fully analyze the situation, a warm mug of coffee is placed in my hands, accompanied by a wide grin and a quick wink and...the sound of Journey's "Don't Stop Believing" emanating from the clock radio on the microwave. Looks like he found an eighties station.

"Good morning, Van," he says.

"This is so fucked up," I reply.

"Is that how you normally say good morning?"

"Normally, there's nobody around to say good morning to." My shock is evident.

His smile grows. "Well, then, 'this is so fucked up' works for me."

After grabbing a mug of coffee for himself, he sits beside me on the couch. I gawk at him like I've never seen a boy drinking coffee before.

"So what's the plan?"

"Huh?" I yawn. It's way too early for questions.

"You know. What's up for today?"

Nobody has asked me what I have planned for the day since I was in grade school. "Why?"

"I'm just being friendly. You know, since we're roommates now."

"Roommates," I repeat, and the world swims before my eyes. I'm momentarily certain I have screwed up my already extremely screwed-up life beyond repair. But now, it's no longer a pathetic situation I have completely under control. Now, my sorry life is tied up with the fate of a near-stranger, who just so happens to have a bunch of serious problems all his own. "I'm...going to school." How did this happen to a loner like me?

"I think I'm going to see if I can get some extra hours at the diner today. I'll leave here at the same time as you."

"Sure, whatever you want."

"And by the way, your bed is great. You really never sleep on it?"

My fear of bedrooms is one of the many things that makes me abnormal. George C would never understand why bedrooms freak me out. I mean, who would? Unless you've had my messed-up experiences with bedrooms, it would be beyond *your* belief, too. "I like sleeping out here, and I don't need to get the third degree about it."

"Well, if you ever want to switch, let me know."

"I won't." I can only manage to take three sips of the coffee. "I've got to get ready for school."

George C watches as I stand and race for the bathroom. "I'll make us toast."

"Good luck with that. I don't have a toaster."

*

I'm sitting alone at lunch, as usual, when Veronica and some girl I've never met plunk their asses on either side of me on the bench. And just like that, I'm surrounded by the enemy. "Maria, this is Van Liss. Van, this is Maria Detoni. Maria's the art director of the Portals Literary Magazine."

"And why do I care?" I ask, but nonetheless find myself shaking Maria's hand.

Veronica laughs. "You're a riot! I told her about your art ability. So, Maria went to the Euro History classroom to check out Rudolf Höss for herself."

"The man's a bastard, but you caught his evil essence. I'm impressed."

I turn toward Maria and gawk. *"What?"* What I really want to ask is, *Don't you know who I am?* And then answer my own question, *I'm 'potentially hazardous to your physical safety' Donovan Liss*. But I don't, because if she knows, she obviously doesn't give a shit.

"Van, we need a sketch of Windsor High School. We're working on coming up with the cover for this year's final issue, and we want it to feature an image of the school through a window. Or maybe a door...or possibly somebody's eyeglasses." Maria shrugs. "You get the *picture?*" She giggles at her own wordplay.

"I draw monsters." Sometimes I draw self-portraits because the rest of the kids at school see *me* as a monster too. But I never draw buildings, not from any perspective.

Again, Veronica laughs. The lighthearted sound jolts me. "You're so funny...but anyway, we're hoping you can bring the picture with you to the after-school meeting of Portals Magazine Club on Friday."

"On Friday?"

"Yeah, that's what I said. The meeting is in room 221. Mrs. Rosen's room in the English wing, right? And we meet at three. Don't be late." Maria squeezes my hand, and I grit my teeth so I don't jump out of my skin.

"See you in Euro History class, Van," Veronica chirps. The girls slide from the bench and head for the lunch line.

"Sure...whatever."

*

George C isn't lurking around my house when I get home after school, waiting to come in. I don't see him until I get to work. He's in the break room, sitting on the purple couch with Walter, and they're flipping through a Journeys catalog together. Nikki, Rhonda, and a waitress about my mother's age named Doris, are standing near the lockers, getting ready for their shifts.

I open my locker door and stick my hat inside, pull my hair into a bun, slip my feet out of my boots and into my sneakers, and tie my apron. Before I have a chance to choose Doris as today's victim, George C speaks up. "Tonight's special is beef stew, Van. Just in case you want to know."

To be honest, this throws me off. I have a routine—I select a victim, sharpen my attitude, and demand to be informed of the daily special. Then I apply lipstick. Every evening, this is how it goes. Until today. "Uh, thank you, George C."

"It was my pleasure." He hops off the couch and scrambles to my side. "I ordered takeout for us tonight... We're going to pick it up at ten past eleven, so be ready to go as soon as your shift ends."

I nod, and like the creature of habit I am, grab the tube of lipstick off my locker's top shelf.

"Thai food, Vanny." He grins and touches my arm. Then he races off to the kitchen.

"Vanny?" I ask myself, but then still my lips so I can apply lipstick.

*

By eleven thirty we're back at the Batcave, sitting beside each other on the couch, eating pad Thai out of the boxes.

"So good, huh?" He licks his lips and places the box on the coffee table, pulls his shaggy, eighty's rocker curls up into a quick ponytail, and then burps sufficiently loud for my mother to hear if she cared enough to listen.

"Excuse you," I say, but I'm not grossed out. I should be, but I'm not.

"How was school?"

I cringe because this is a little too much like "how was your day, dear?" for comfort. "Good except for lunch."

"What happened at lunch?"

"This girl and her friend asked me to draw a picture of our school for the literary magazine."

"And—the problem part?"

"I only draw monsters. I already told you that." I roll my eyes.

George C licks his plastic fork and drops it into the box, stands, and goes into my room. Or his room. Whatever. When he comes out, he's carrying my sketchbook.

"What are you doing?" I'm barely able to control the burning of my cheeks and the volume of my voice. I grit my teeth as a last resort.

He ignores my question and opens it on his lap. "You've got to admit, this picture of me...it's not what you'd call a monster image."

I'd be a liar if I insisted he resembles a monster of any sort—in real life or in my portrait of him. Let's face it: George C more closely resembles a boy angel garden statue. I don't argue.

He starts flipping through the other images. "In some of these, you added a little background. Like, take this round furry thing with super long arms. There's a sort of Gothic building behind him."

I shrug. "Maybe sometimes my monsters are set in richly designed surroundings. It means nothing."

"And this one..." We gaze at a monster that more resembles a lobster than a human being. "There's a beach shack and a bridge on the side. And they seem as real as the monsters."

"Your point?"

"You could sketch your school building if you wanted to."

I grab our two almost empty boxes of Thai food. "I'll close these up and stick them in the mini-fridge for tomorrow night." I'm not going to tell you I didn't hear him. I heard every damned word. But I need to let new ideas sink in gradually. I can't rush the absorption process. "And thanks for dinner."

George C smiles, and I'm pretty sure he understands why I changed the subject. I appreciate that he lets it go. "I feel guilty taking your bed."

"That's ridiculous. I've already told you I don't sleep in there."

My houseguest—or maybe you could call him my roommate—gets up and heads toward the bedroom, but stops, returns to the couch and picks up my sketch pad. He takes it to me and says, "Maybe you should try drawing a couple of buildings tonight, *Van*-cent *Van* Gogh."

"Not funny," I reply, but snatch the sketch pad from his hand and plant my ass on the couch.

I sit in the corner of the couch for a long time trying to decide how to go about drawing something that isn't in some way grotesque. I imagine the high school building— the pale gray brick and the white-paned windows, the winding walkways and trees scattered here and there. The scene is so clear in my mind's eye; I don't think I'd need a photograph to create its spitting image on paper. When I start drawing, though, it isn't Windsor Academy that takes shape on the page. It's the house in Leighton where everything happened—or didn't happen, which is more accurate. But it's where I became the untouchable person I am today.

And then I'm in that bedroom...with the robin's-egg blue walls and the posters of Superman and Batman and Captain America on the ceiling, gazing down on me. Superheroes who never protected me when I needed them.

It's dark and cold and quiet. I'm tucked in the twin-sized bed I pushed against the window because the window is the only possible escape from the shoebox of a bedroom that's already closing in on me. Mom's at work tonight, so all I can do is wait. It won't be long.

The invasion starts with a thin crack of light streaming into my room from the hallway...and the door hesitantly opens. It creaks when you open it all at once; Jake long ago learned that he needed to push it gently. He thinks he can sneak up on me, but he can't because I know how badly he wants...what he wants.

I've awaited this invasion for at least an hour in the darkness, wondering how I'll escape tonight. It's almost a relief when the door opens halfway and the enormous body turns and steps sideways into the room. But it's only a relief because the terrible waiting is over.

I know why Jake is here. I've known for a long time now...like, since I was ten and he moved in with us. I hate everything about what happens in the dark. In the light of day, I never let my brain think of what happens at night. Every time I see his face in my head, I blink twice and make him go away. It's a rule I made, and I'm good at following rules—two blinks and Jake is gone. During the day...

But on the nights Mom works, I get so nervous. I can't eat dinner. Or do my homework. Or fall asleep. I can hardly breathe... And maybe I'm more than nervous; maybe I'm terrified.

Jake's all the way in the room now. I smell his spiciness and hear his breath escaping in heavy gasps. The bright hall light behind him turns Jake into a wide shadow—a monster in my room. I squeeze my eyes shut and grit my teeth. One time, I screamed—it was on the first night he came to me—and he got mad and hit my face five times, each time harder than the last. The next morning when Mom saw the bruises, I told her I fell out of bed. I'm not sure she believed me, but she didn't ask questions. I never scream anymore when he comes to me at night. I grit my teeth instead.

I know when he's beside my bed, even though he thinks I'm asleep, and he's slipped into my room with me unaware. He stands above me and stares. His gaze is as heavy as his breathing—it presses me down into the mattress. When he sighs, loud and long, it means he's found the nerve to act. And when his fingers spread out in my hair, and he starts to rub my head and say my name over and over, I keep my eyes closed. I turn on my side and face the window, knowing soon I'll open my eyes and stare outside into the darkness. Into the freedom where I can fly alone.

Jake is so big, huge really, and when he eases himself down on the edge of my bed, I find myself falling backward into him. His breath whooshes onto the back of my neck, hot and needy. Goose bumps I don't want rise on my skin. It doesn't take long until he's pushing against me, and the heat on my neck turns into wetness.

A shaky voice says, "No, Jake." And it's my voice, but I don't remember getting up the courage to speak.

Jake's mad at me now...I know it. There's anger in his hands—in the way he grabs my sides and drags me against him.

"I want it, Van," he murmurs into my ear, but it's too late. I'm changing. I'm halfway a rock already... I'm solid and hard and cold and lost to him.

After I turn all the way into stone, he never wants to stay. He hates Van the rock, and he shows me how much with his voice. "You're my boy, Donovan, and don't forget it. I can have you when I want you. Any time I want you..."

My eyes are open wide, staring out the window into the night sky. I try to count the stars. But it's impossible to count them all.

"Van...you're having a bad dream." The light behind the couch is on. The sketch pad is open on my lap. And George C kneels in front of me, gazing at me like he cares. His ponytail elastic is hanging on the loose ends of his long dark hair.

He's a person I know—the boy with puppy dog eyes. He's not a huge shadow in the dark with heated desires.

"It was a trance," I say. "Not a dream."

"Are you okay now?"

"Yes. I get like that sometimes...when I draw."

We both glance down at the sketch pad. "You drew a room."

"It's a bedroom."

"Yeah..." He likely wants to ask me why I sketched a bedroom in my trance, but he can't ask too many questions unless he's willing to answer mine. "You were counting when I came in."

"I was counting the stars."

"Were you in that bedroom—" He places a finger on the sketch. "—when you were counting stars?"

I put my finger beside his. "I was on this bed...looking out the window."

"Were you a kid...you know, were you a little boy, in your trance?"

"Uh-huh. I'm always a child in my trances."

"And..." He pulls in a deep breath. "Were you alone in your bedroom? In your bed?"

Oh, God, he wants to know if I was alone in my bed. If I answer, I'll be opening myself to another person. "No. I was with the monster."

George C climbs onto the couch. He wraps himself around my body, and I let him... *I let him*. He doesn't breathe on my neck. He doesn't press against me. He just holds on. After what seems like an hour, he reaches up and turns off the light. Then he holds me tighter. And I let him, and I like it.

Wednesday

THIS MORNING IS stranger than yesterday morning was. There's no coffee brewing when I open my eyes, but there's a boy. Either I'm in his arms or he's in mine—it's too damned hard to say which. I don't think it matters very much.

My sketch pad is on the floor a few feet from the couch. I wonder how it got so far from my lap. It's still open to the drawing of my childhood bedroom.

George C moves; he's awake. I snatch my hand from his so he knows I'm awake too.

"Van, you're gonna be late to school."

I glance at the clock radio on the microwave. "It's ten. I've already missed a class and a half."

"You'd better get there soon, before you miss the whole day. Do you need a note from your mother explaining why you're late?"

"I'll just email the school and tell them I'm sick today and sign Mom's name. They won't question it."

"I'll make coffee."

I don't say cool. Or thanks. Or anything at all. I simply extricate myself from our body-tangle and find my computer. I concoct a feeble story about a terrible headache and send it to the office at Windsor Academy. They won't wonder whether my mother wrote the email or if I forged it. They won't care. Nobody will miss me. Some people will probably be relieved I don't show up. But now I have another problem to face. George C lives here, so I can't spend the day alone. Which means I'm going to have to be nice.

"How does leftover pad Thai sound for breakfast?" he asks.

I don't answer him. I can't because I just remembered he's aware of my secret, and I'm freaking out. To the tune of sweating and panting. Plus, I'm annoyed that I don't know any of his secrets. I suspect there are many.

Ignoring me as I recover from my panic attack, George C goes about the business of heating up last night's leftovers. And pouring me a mug of coffee. And serving me. It's like he's taking care of me. I love it as much as I hate it. I sigh, thinking how screwed up I am—how screwed up everything is. But still, I sit on the couch beside him, and I eat the damned Thai food and drink all of my coffee. I even want to smile after I suck down the last drop, rather than smirk evilly, which is what I'm known for. I want to smile at him the way a little kid would smile in awe at a superhero.

"Want to do something fun today, Van?"

"Something fun? You and me—like, together?" He has no idea how preposterous this notion is to me, the scarecrow loner.

"Sure. I've got an idea. Let me surprise you."

"This is so fucked up."

George C laughs. It's not a making-fun-of-Van-the–loner-weirdo kind of snicker. It's a you're-so-adorable chuckle. It's warm. It tells me he likes me.

So I say it again, in a slightly different form. "Seriously, you have no idea how messed up this is—you know, that we're gonna hang out together all day."

"Maybe I don't care." He stands and takes the mug from my hand and the empty food boxes from the coffee table. "Go take a shower."

I nod, thinking nobody tells me what to do.

"I washed the clothes you lent me and put them on your bureau last night. But can I borrow them again? All my other stuff is in my locker at work."

I nod again, dumbfounded by what's happening to my simple, empty, ice-cold life. "You're gonna wear pink sweatpants in public?"

"Sure, why not? I'll shower after you. Let's get this show on the road."

Like a zombie, I float toward the bathroom and into the shower.

*

We take a city bus to the Local Fine Art Museum of Windsor, which is located in one of the restored mill buildings on the bank of the Lange River. I've never been here before. If I have a few free hours or the need to get out of my lonely house, I usually go to bookstores to browse in an effort to impersonate a real human being. But this is new. I hate that I'm so excited.

"How do you even know about this place?" I ask as we wander through the gallery of sculptures.

"It's a good place to hide." He's staring at a rock that calls itself a sculpture but has no identifiable shape. I think of how in my trances I sometimes turn to stone.

"You need to hide a lot," I tell him.

"Understatement of the year." He laughs, but I'm having none of it.

"Why? And what are you hiding from?"

Instead of answering the question I asked, he answers one I didn't. "I've only been hiding since I moved here. I used to live near Hancock. I didn't hide back then."

"What changed?"

"The circumstances of my life."

Well, if that isn't a vague answer, I don't know what is. And he doesn't have to tell me to butt out of his business twice.

"Let's find the paintings." I go off in search of art not made of rock, and he follows.

I like the paintings that resemble things I recognize because I understand how they're supposed to fit into the world. I can judge them better and figure out what the artist was thinking when he created them. I especially like art depicting regular things like books and chairs and bowls of fruit.

"Hey, Van, this artist does buildings," he calls from across the room.

"So what?" I ask, even though I'm sure this is his less than subtle way of encouraging me to draw a picture of my high school for the literary magazine.

"Come check 'em out."

I don't walk to where he stands for at least two minutes. He can't think I'm eager, and neither can I. And neither should you.

"You could draw some pictures like this. Probably better than these."

I study the barns, and then the farmhouses, and finally the churches in the paintings. I close my eyes. In my mind's eye, Windsor Academy is right in front of me. I can draw it.

We linger in front of a huge charcoal sketch of an outhouse until I move on to portraits of people. There is no monster-art anywhere.

*

I can tell he wants to hold my hand. You're wondering how on earth I can tell, aren't you? Let me explain: nobody has held onto my hand since I was five years old—mostly to stop me from running out onto a street and getting plowed down by a pickup truck. But George C doesn't want to protect me from oncoming cars; he thinks we bonded in the art gallery. That we're closer now, and this calls for some physical deal-sealing. Neither of us has any clue what I'd do if he actually tried it.

George C nudges me with his shoulder as we walk down the street. Over and over again our shoulders rub together. I let him do it, and sometimes, I nudge him back. It's the best I can do in the physical connection department. Maybe it's very *middle school*, but he appears cool with it.

"Should we buy some microwavable meals? We can cook them at your place and then watch a movie on your computer."

"I have to work at five." It's only two and there's no rush to get to work. But it seems like my obligation to at least *try* to throw a wrench in his plans.

"I do too." Without another word, I follow him into the next convenience store we come across. We split the cost of a couple of meatloaf and mashed potato frozen dinners and a liter of Dr. Pepper.

As we exit the store, George C's eyes get wide and dark and scared. It's like he morphs from a chill dude into scared kid. I follow his gaze down the street. There's a boy, maybe a few years younger than us, leaning up against an older guy in the entryway of an unoccupied building. They're chatting. They're flirting. Their hands touch. Their bodies come together.

George C freezes. He touches his lip that's not so swollen anymore. He slides his hand beneath the white T-shirt he wears and, I assume, explores the cuts there with his fingertips.

"Do you know that kid?" I ask.

He shakes his head, and then he shrugs. "Sort of, but not really."

"Then why are you staring?"

He shrugs again.

"Is that kid a drug dealer or something?" And suddenly it hits me. Hard. Like a two by four to the temple. George C is a drug dealer. He owes some bad dude big money, which is why those two thugs are after him. "Is there something you want to tell me?" All I need is a kingpin drug czar staking him out at my house. Mom and Jake would boot me out along with George C, and I'm not quite ready to make it on my own.

George C impulsively decides to cross the street. A minivan is forced to screech to a stop so it doesn't hit him.

If we were holding hands I could have prevented his near-death experience, but I can't turn back time. Like a fool, though, I follow him to the other side of the street. *He's got the bag of food,* I rationalize. *I'll go hungry if I don't stick with him.* But I really don't know why I follow him. I hope it's not because I'm starting to get soft.

Once we're walking on Depot Street, a few blocks from my house, I push him against the outside wall of a dry cleaner and ask, "What the fuck was that all about?" I'm pissed off. He can't make me feel all kinds of warm emotions and then go do something stupid like killing himself.

His face twists. He crouches down. He's scared...of me. I can tell because lots of people are scared of my attitude. But it cuts me deeply that George C has those fearful eyes when he looks at me. "I'm not a drug dealer," he squeaks.

"Okay," I say, letting myself believe him so easily. It's all he offers me in the way of an explanation of his strange behavior on the street in front of the convenience store. But it's good enough for me.

Mom and Jake are still at work when we arrive at the duplex. We don't have to sneak inside, but I unlock the door at the top of the stairs and lock it behind us because things have changed since George C moved in. Part of me gets that he needs protection, and maybe I can give it to him. I resist the urge to say aloud, once again, how screwed up my life has become.

We microwave our meals and then meet on the couch. I pull my laptop from beneath the coffee table, and he says, "I want to watch *Friends*." Then I find the episode with the prom video—my personal favorite—and we watch and eat like we're friends. We even doze off for about an hour and have to break our asses to get to work on time.

It's all so fucked up.

*

Work is work. Nothing monumental occurs, except again, George C personally details today's special for me before I have a chance to choose a victim.

We decide on PBJs for a late-night snack, so we don't stop anywhere on our way home.

But Mom is lurking in the shared entryway when we come in. And she has questions.

"Who's this?" She moves in front of us so we can't get up the stairs and points at George C with her thumb. Her pointy thumbnail comes dangerously close to his chin.

"Why do you care?" My best bet is to answer her question with another question. Take my word for it, reader, if you're at a loss for a snarky comeback, go with another question.

George C shifts his weight from one foot to the other, uncomfortable with the obvious hostility in our exchange.

"Well, is he a friend?"

I just stare at her.

"Because I won't believe it if you try to tell me you have a friend."

"I work with him. Can we get by now?"

"Jake isn't gonna like it, Donovan."

I grit my teeth. "Ask me if I care."

"You two better not make any noise up there."

"We wouldn't dream of it."

Mom steps to the side and lets us pass.

When we're on the second floor, he asks, "So that was your mom?"

"Yup." I don't apologize for not introducing them. I didn't even like Mom having the chance to meet him. As far as I'm concerned, she'll never learn his name.

"You look a lot like her." Mom is tall and skinny and does her best to stay blonde, but *her* roots are gray. She also has suffering eyes. Not quite as light as mine, but they catch people's attention. They caught Jake's perverted eye.

"I guess so."

"But Jake isn't your father?"

"No—he's Mom's boyfriend. My father is a big no-show in my life. I've never even met him."

"My dad let me down too. He was around—but not *around* in ways I needed him. You know?" My ears perk up because George C doesn't volunteer much information about himself or his life. "You don't think your mother has a problem with me staying here?"

"She doesn't know you'll be here for more than a night."

"Why did she say Jake wouldn't like it?"

"I guess he's got his reasons."

George C nods, recognizing he's hit a wall. "Well, we better not make any noise."

"Fuck him. I'll make all the noise I want." But I don't. I'm happy to just disappear from their lives. I don't need to fight them anymore.

We make four sandwiches, and then I change out of my scarecrow attire and into sweats before sitting down to eat. George C's backpack is full tonight, and I think maybe he's brought some of his stuff from his work locker here. The best defense against my emerging smile is a nasty scowl. George C doesn't seem to notice.

Once we're planted on the couch eating, I tell him, "I have an extra plastic bin in the closet in my room. You can use it for your stuff."

"Yeah?" His cheeks turn pink like he's embarrassed by my generosity.

"It's no big deal."

"I appreciate it." When we finish eating, he hands me my sketch pad from off the coffee table. He doesn't say anything; he leaves me to my thoughts as he takes our plates, rinses them in the bathroom, and goes to bed.

I'm reluctant to draw. I usually end up in a trance, and I'm really not in the mood to freak out, which always ends up happening. But the spark of hope I can accomplish something important like creating a cover for a literary magazine won't extinguish, even when I grit my teeth. So I close my eyes, picture Windsor Academy in my mind, and let myself go.

Maybe school buildings don't cause me the kind of emotional stress that pulls me into art-trances, because I draw the school without losing control. It comes out more decently than I figured, and I'm surprised. I'm not going to admit to being proud of it, but I can't wait to show Veronica and Maria at the meeting after school on Friday.

I want to show it to George C too. I want to say thank you to him for encouraging me, but I never will.

Thursday

GEORGE C GETS up with me, makes us coffee, and checks out my drawing of Windsor Academy, which I left faceup on the coffee table. He doesn't gush all over the place at how awesome it is. He just gawks at me with raised eyebrows, suggesting he knew I could do it.

"Think it's okay if I stay here while you're at school? I won't run water or flush the toilet or come and go. I'll be perfectly silent."

"That should be fine." I want to tell him I don't care what Mom and Jake think of me having a houseguest, but the truth is, they pay the rent, and I have to live by whatever rules they set up. It's probably best not to give them any reason to set rules about George C.

"Nobody will know I'm here."

I'll know it. But I kind of like knowing he's here. "I'd better get going."

"What time will you be home?"

Home. He called the Batcave his home. "By three. I'll bring food."

"Cool."

I go into my room and notice my bed is neatly made and a bin in the corner is halfway filled with George C's stuff. A warm feathery feeling I'm not used to fills my gut. Before I can dwell on it, I grab a plaid flannel shirt and some worn-out denim overalls from my bureau and head for the bathroom to get showered and dressed like I'll be stiff in a field, scaring off crows all day.

*

The vice principal calls me to his office about twice a month. Even though I keep my distance from all of the other kids at school, when something goes missing or when someone gets bullied, all eyes are focused on me. I guess the adults in charge figure that even if I didn't do it, I probably know who did.

But they're wrong on both accounts. I don't like people because I can't trust them. It doesn't mean I want to swipe somebody's stupid two-hundred-dollar basketball sneakers or I'd get any satisfaction from threatening some loser on Facebook. I may seem like the kind of kid to do bad shit, but the fact is, my nose is clean.

Mrs. Manter, the office secretary, ushers me into Mr. Hench's office with a pinched-face smile, and I drop my messenger bag beside my usual chair and sit. Hench always keeps me waiting for a few minutes. He thinks the waiting makes me nervous and probably more likely to spill my guts. Wrong again.

"Hello, Mr. Liss. Thank you for coming to see me."

Like I had a choice...I just think it. "What's up this time, Mr. Hench?"

"I think you know." He sits behind his desk and leans forward. This movement is supposed to intimidate me. It doesn't.

"I'm going to need more info. I have no clue what you're talking about."

He sighs and shakes his head. "This time, we have witnesses."

"Witnesses to what?"

"Three students informed the office that you were the one to pull the fire alarm in the hallway near the gym yesterday."

"It wasn't me."

"It *was* you. Nobody with eyes could confuse you for somebody else. Look at yourself! Your hair, your clothes...it was you."

I stand and grab my bag. Our meeting will soon conclude. "I was absent from school yesterday, Mr. Hench, so somebody's lying. And *I* have a witness I was with all day. I wasn't here."

"I...I, didn't check the attendance records...uh, sit down, and I'll ask Mrs. Manter to confirm your story."

"I'm missing math."

"Sit down, young man." His voice is firm, but he's pink-faced now and fumbles with some papers on his desk before he leaves me alone in the room. Maybe the man is actually embarrassed about falsely accusing me of yet another school crime, and is trying to save face by playing the tough guy.

I drop into the chair and wait. Normally, being treated like the student-most-likely-to- fuck-someone-over wouldn't faze me. But, today, I'm kind of pissed off about it. Or maybe it's something else I'm feeling.

And maybe I'm not in the mood to tell you about it.

Five minutes later, Mr. Hench returns and, without glancing at me, says, "I don't want to see you in this office again, Mr. Liss."

Well, then, don't call me here, I don't say. Some battles can't be won. And I know it.

You're getting the picture too, aren't you? You've come to realize I just can't win any of life's smaller battles. It makes my chance of winning the war look pretty grim, huh?

*

I practically run home, and I hate myself for it. I rush up the stairs, unlock the door, and push my way in. George C is lounging on my couch, reading a book from my rickety bookshelf in the corner. "I love graphic novels, dude. And you have a great collection—every superhero graphic novel ever written, I bet."

I'm smacked in the face with a splash of intense emotion. Mom and Jake wish I would disappear and take along with me all of *their* baggage *I'm* blamed for, everybody at school is afraid of me, and most of my coworkers at the diner would like nothing better than to see me fall flat on my face on the greasy floor in front of the breakfast bar. But maybe I hoped *somebody* along the way would fight me as I worked so hard to alienate myself from the world. Maybe someone would say, "Van isn't so bad after all" and welcome me somewhere...*anywhere.* And here in my living room is a person, totally new in my life, who can see *me*—not the creepy scarecrow character I've created to keep the world at bay.

I crumple to the floor on the spot. My stupid feet just won't hold me up any longer. George C bounces off the couch and is at my side within a split second. "Hey, man, you okay?"

I can't talk. I can barely breathe. I cover my head, humiliated. Why can't I just disappear like the world wants?

He grabs my hands from off my head and drags me to my feet. Then he leads me to the couch. "Sit with me, Van."

I sit beside him on the couch and fight the urge to cry, an urge I haven't experienced for years. It's easy to see: My frozen self has melted into a puddle of dirty water. And for some godforsaken reason, I'm as thrilled as I am furious about it. Don't ask for an explanation because I've got nothing... When George C pulls me against him, I don't bat him away like an angry kitten. I let it happen. I fold into him willingly.

"Sometimes you've gotta just let go, Van. Let the tears come if you want...and then do what's harder, let your truth out."

He's giving me the okay to share my pain. And I want to. I'm like a lonely child, clinging to the only person in the world who gives me the time of day. The only person who gives a shit. "It's so insane...how I ended up like this."

"Shit happens, and that's how we all end up where we are."

I sniff hard to stop the tears that threaten. "Nothing bad actually ever happened...which is the most messed up part. I was just so scared. All the time."

"Then something bad happened. If somebody scared you, it *is* real. Fear is the thing that happened."

Believe it or not, reader, it feels so good that he's listening to me I keep going with my sob story. Minus the literal sobbing. "He came to my room, like, every night. He wanted to do things to me...but he also wanted my *permission* to do them, probably so he wouldn't feel like such a perv. I never gave it and he never forced me. So why the hell am I like this?"

After blurting out the truth of what I lived with from the time Jake moved in—until we moved here last year and I got some space—I'm shell-shocked. I shake my head as I try to evaluate which is more powerful—my relief or my regret at having told him. George C loosens his hold on my shoulders just enough to lean away and study my face. "Are you talking about your mother's boyfriend?"

I stop shaking my head and start to nod. "He never stopped pushing me...for years. Whenever Mom worked at night, he came to my room. But he wanted me to give it to him...to show I wanted it too...and I always refused."

"That's way too much pressure for a kid to live with. And you were a minor, Van—you couldn't have given your permission, even if he thought it would have made a difference."

"I think that shit broke me, George C." I'm giving away the store here. "I'm so broken."

He pulls me back and, like a bowl of Jell-O, not the stone-cold loner I try so hard to be, I sag against his side. "You're not broken."

"No, I really am. I'm so fucked up."

"Nah, Van. Jake is fucked up."

I shrug.

"Did you tell your mom what was going on?"

"I tried. She didn't believe me."

"Then she's fucked up, too. Not you. You just reacted to their fucked-up shit."

This notion has crossed my mind a thousand times, but for it to come from the lips of somebody else, I actually hear it. It starts to sink into my brain. But I can't talk about it anymore. At this point, I need time to let this knowledge become part of me.

George C seems to understand my silence. "Let's read together for a while, 'kay?"

"Yeah…that'd be good. And I've got sandwiches in my bag I picked up at the Subway near school." I don't want to leave his side to retrieve my bag from where I dropped it by the door. I'm warm and comfortable and I want to read with him.

"Let's check out *Watchmen* for a while before we eat."

Watchmen is my all-time favorite graphic novel. I've escaped into it many times. "Okay." There are two hours left before we have to be at work. It's plenty of time for me to recover from soul spilling and rebuild my armor so I can again face the world.

He pulls the book out from where it's tucked between two couch cushions. Then he opens it, and I disappear into a sci-fi comic adventure that's so much less complicated than real life.

Friday

IT'S ALMOST IMPOSSIBLE for me to accept that I'm here in room 221 in the high school's English wing at the

Portals Literary Magazine meeting. Being here, in itself, flies in the face of everything I've been striving to establish since I made the decision at twelve that being alone was safe and anything else put me at grave risk. And being here with the sketch of Windsor Academy tucked into my Euro History notebook is probably reckless—it proves I care. It confirms my very human need for approval. So what the hell am I doing here? If you know, do me a favor and share your wisdom; I'm completely clueless at this juncture.

At three o'clock precisely, Veronica moves to the front of the classroom. The seven literary magazine writers and editors snap to attention. This club is serious business to them. Not a joke at all.

"Today, a new member has joined us. Please say hello to Van Liss. You may not know this about him, but he's a quite talented artist. Today, he will unveil the image of Windsor Academy that will grace the cover of the year-end issue of Portals Literary Magazine."

I'm a new member? When did this happen?

All eight students flash varying degrees of smiles at me in hesitant welcome. Maria, however, is grinning, smug in the knowledge my ability in the art department is beyond "quite talented." Instead of offering my nose-scratch bird-flip, I wave sarcastically. In my defense, it's less lame than waving enthusiastically.

My tentative plan had been to fling the picture of the school I drew onto the floor and say, "Use it for your stupid magazine if it floats your boat. Or use it for kindling. I don't give a shit." And then I was to storm out of room 221 without looking back. But the relief with which every last one of the Portals staff is gazing at me foils my plan.

"Maria and Veronica told us about your sketch of Rudolf Höss. Believe me, I'm no fan of his, but they said he appeared scary and evil and real—like he could jump off the page." This high compliment, I think, comes from Dania Weiss, a sophomore who is reputed to be her class's future valedictorian by a wide margin.

"Well, I'm a pro at drawing monsters," I mutter.

"Thanks for coming today. If you weren't here, they were gonna make me illustrate. And I'm barely capable of stick figures," says a tall, skinny boy with thick black glasses and an enormous Afro. I don't think I've ever seen him before, although I'm not sure how I missed him. "I'm Alex Kingston." He actually gets up out of his seat and comes over to shake my hand. "Seriously, Van. Huge thanks for coming."

I shake his hand, only because I'm caught off guard.

Another boy stands and turns to stare at me. This guy—outfitted in a pink polo shirt with its collar popped, neat khakis, and a frigging whale belt—is one of those preppy assholes who would rather not share space on earth with oddballs like me. "I don't care if you *are* a potential school shooter, I need a drawing of a dog for my poem called 'Laddie, Come Home.' Can you deliver, Ice Queen?"

Everybody in the room gasps. Even me, because *that* was unexpected.

Veronica jumps in, "Tad, sit down. You're out of line."

He drops into his seat but growls, "What? We've all heard the rumors about him..."

Despite my hours of practice in facial-temperature-control, my cheeks burn. "I *so* don't need this." I grab my notebook and messenger bag and stand. "I'm outta here."

However, all eight of the literary club members rush to the door to block my exit, Tad included. He grimaces, then steps forward and grabs my arm. "Look, Liss, I'm sorry. Sometimes, my mouth gets ahead of my brain, and I...just say things."

Well, this is something I can relate to. I say a lot of shit I probably shouldn't too. I brush his hand off my arm. "I'm not going to shoot up the school, the library, or anywhere else. That's not me."

"Good to know," he says and wipes his brow with feigned relief. "Why don't you show us your sketch of the school, huh?"

I step to a desk and the Portals staff crowds around. From my notebook, I slide out the sketch of Windsor Academy.

I drew it from the perspective of a person looking through the front window curtains of the house across the street. They all gawk.

Maria coughs. No, maybe she's choking. I have no clue whether this is a positive or negative sign for my picture, or if I should suggest that somebody attempt the Heimlich maneuver on the girl. I stiffen my spine, preparing for anything.

A tiny girl with bright red hair and more freckles on her face than I could count if I had an entire afternoon to dedicate to the task, speaks up first. "Where have you been all year? This is perfect. I mean, beggars can't be choosers, but this kind of art is just what we need."

"I'm on the same page as you, Mandy." Veronica pulls a sheet of paper out of her back pocket and unfolds it. She places it on the desk beside the sketch. "Sign this, Van. In blood, preferably."

"What is it?" I ask, quite wary, as you may have predicted.

"It's the Portals Literary Magazine staff contract. Everybody here has signed it, and you need to sign it too."

Normally I'd ask, *What if I don't want to?* But I surprise myself, and probably everybody else, because I don't. "Anybody got a pen? I'm not up for donating blood today."

Eight pens are shoved in my face. I choose a red one. "Closest to blood," I quip. And like I was born yesterday, I lean down and sign the document without reading it. The magazine staff actually claps as a single, relieved unit after I dot the *i* in Liss. "Now, maybe someone can tell me in what ways I've signed my life away."

"Let go back to our seats and get to work." Again, Veronica takes charge, ignoring my request.

As we return to our seats, Tad murmurs, "You've basically signed away your Friday afternoons from now until graduation. I even get out of soccer practice on Fridays to come to meetings." He jabs me in the gut with his elbow and winks.

I haven't been part of any official group since quitting Little League in fifth grade. It was getting too hard to find grown-ups to drive me back and forth. And most of the other kids had their fathers at the field, encouraging them. I was alone as alone gets, and I wore the aloneness like heavy armor, literally struggling beneath its weight. I never managed to blend with the other kids.

Don't bother shedding tears for me, reader; I sucked at baseball, anyway.

But it looks like I'm a joiner now. And since I don't have a compartment for this in my brain, I just sit and take it all in.

The human freezer pop is melting. And I don't know if I like it.

Part Two: George C

How I see it

A LOT HAS happened over the past few months.

That sounds kind of cryptic, so let me explain. What I mean is, a ton of mostly bad change has gone down in my life since I graduated from high school. So much has gone down that I'm a different person than before I left home last summer. Which may be a good thing.

But I had to leave—it wasn't really much of a choice. According to Mom, I'm an "irredeemable screwup." And, *What are you, some kind of fag?* was becoming the question my father most often asked me, not that he ever paid particularly astute attention to his only son. I never came back with, *Maybe I* am *gay, Dad.* I never asked, *What are you gonna do about it?* I never asked, because I knew the answer. One way or another, I had to leave.

I can't afford to screw off anymore. If I don't take life seriously now, I'll probably end up kicking the bucket. It actually *is* this simple. No work means no food and shelter. No food and shelter means George starves or freezes to death this coming winter.

Sad but totally true. Huh, reader?

Friday

AND SO I lie here on Van's couch, my feet sticking off the armrest, listening to the branches of the neighborhood's only tree scraping against the living room window. Even if it sounds kind of creepy—and even if everybody else at the restaurant thinks *Van* is kind of creepy—I'm safe here. It's been a while since I've felt safe.

Van's a weird sort of dude, but he's not the psychopath most everybody else sees when they look at him. He's just scared. More scared than me, even, which says a lot. I'm not sure about the specifics of what happened to him to make him so fragile—to make him need to be alone even when he doesn't *want* to be. But whatever it is, it went down in the bedroom he drew in his sketch pad.

Maybe it *is* as simple as a child's fear and a mother's refusal to acknowledge it.

All I do is shrug, even though I'd really like to do something to understand him better. I slide off the couch and go to the sink in the tiny bathroom. I brush my teeth, thinking that Van is going to be home soon, and I want my breath to be fresh. Not that it matters because Van will never get close enough to smell the wintergreen.

Troubled eyes stare back at me from the mirror above the sink. I remember when the expression in my eyes was challenging. "Disobedient," Mom said. "Too big for my britches," Dad said. "Suspended," my school vice principal said too many times. I'm lucky I managed to graduate.

I'm not a defiant teenager anymore. Shit happened, and now I'm preoccupied. With what, you want to know? You're going to have to figure it out for yourself. I'm not going to lay all the answers out for you like a losing hand in a blackjack game. *Hee-hee*...maybe there's a little "naughty" left in this boy after all.

"George C?"

I love how he calls me George C, even when we're not at work. It's sort of stiff and formal, just like Van.

"In here." I rinse my face and dry it off with the towel I hung over the bathroom door this morning. "Did you go to the literary magazine meeting? Did you show them the drawing of the school?"

Van drops his bag on the floor beside the couch, examines me warily, and nods.

"What was that look for?" I ask.

He shrugs. "I'm not used to people asking me questions about what I do."

"Your face is turning red."

Van's hands rise to either side of his face. "No, it's not."

"Awww—you're blushing because you're so glad I care." Yeah, I'm teasing him now. What can I say? It's fun.

Van drops onto the couch. "Whatever... I showed them the picture of the school."

"They went crazy over it, huh?"

"Well, yeah." He leans over and pulls a notebook out of his bag and starts flipping through, glancing at rushed sketches done in red pen he must have come up with at the meeting today. "And they've all got demands for other things they want me to draw. I'm going to be fucking busy."

"Well, we've got an hour before work, so I'll let you get to it."

Van shoves his notebook under the couch and studies his dark purple fingernails. "Uh...nah, I don't need to do it right now."

"What do you want to do instead?"

Van stands and walks to the window. "It's windy today, huh?"

"Sure is." I go stand beside him. I want to put my hand on his shoulder, but I'm afraid he might bite it. "Want to read together?"

He yawns. It's very deliberate and is accompanied by a wide stretch. "Um…yeah. Why the hell not?" He goes to the little bookshelf and grabs a hardcover called *Batman: Hush*. "This one's my other favorite."

I think the two of us are bonding over graphic novels. It's slow going and a little bit grueling, but I think it's happening. I'm relieved. Or maybe it's more than relief… It's like I won something. "I've had my eye on that one too."

Again, I receive a strange glance.

"Let's sit on the couch and read," I suggest.

He turns toward the boring beige couch. It sags a little bit in the middle, as, from what I gather, Van sleeps on it all the time. "Should I get us drinks?" he asks.

"After we read for a while, we can make coffee. Cool?"

Van nods, and we sit next to each other on one side of the couch. When we catch eyes, there's a zing of connection. I think Van's zinging too because he jolts away from me like he got zapped by a bolt of electricity.

The truth is, I'm into Van. If he were any other guy, I would have made a move by now. But Van is different than most dudes I know. It's like he's wearing invisible body armor, and even if I gathered the courage to put my hand on his knee, he wouldn't be able to feel it. He's also sophisticated—with his aloof behavior and strange fashion sense—but at the same time, he's sort of innocent. I'm not about to tell him that. He'd definitely bite me, and not in the good way.

And then there's the sexual stuff I did over the past month. I'm sort of filthy now.

I open the book and he leans into me. He smells sweeter than I expect. Sometimes, Van seems like the coldest person I know, but his arm is warm against mine. It distracts me. I clear my throat and read out loud, pointing to the best parts of the illustrations. He moves closer.

I read until my throat is dry. And then I keep reading, because every few minutes, Van moves a little bit closer. After half an hour, it's almost like we're cuddling on the couch, and I wish we didn't have to go to work. He's so enchanted with the book he doesn't realize how far he has let his guard down.

I close the book, and we're quiet for a while.

"Want coffee, George C?" he finally asks.

"Sure. Let me make it—you've been at school all day, and I've been hanging out here, being lazy."

It's hard to force myself off the couch, away from his warm side, but I do. As I make coffee, I decide I'm going to go for it. I'm going to try to get a kiss from Van tonight after work.

A kiss is just a kiss. It won't change anything between us, really. I'll still be on my own, and he'll still be stiff and cold. It's not enough for him to catch my dirtiness. It's just a kiss. But it would be nice.

*

Work was crazy, start to finish. By the time I finish scraping down the grill, I'm greasy and exhausted. When I go into the break room, Van is pulling his apron off.

"Long night, huh, Vanny?" I ask him from the doorway.

"Are you seriously talking to the freezer pop that way?" Walter never knows when to shut up.

"I am," I reply. "Why? Are you jealous?" The expression in his eyes says maybe he is, which is enough to seal Walter's lips. But my attention is more on Van's lips. He's smirking. He likes how I put Walter in his place. "You must have cashed in tonight, dude."

"I did okay." When I get close enough for him to speak to only me, he adds, "Carlo said I could make milkshakes for us at closing, as long as I clean the blender and the counter."

"How did you know the way to my heart is through a straw? I love milkshakes!"

It's kind of dark in the break room, but I'd bet my life Van's cheeks are pink.

I follow him into the kitchen where he whips up three large vanilla milkshakes. "Part of the deal was I promised to make Carlo a shake too," he says as he rinses the blender. "Come on, let's give it to him, and he can unlock the door to let us out."

Carlo is thrilled to have a milkshake. "This is great! You two make a good team." He waggles his eyebrows, and Van seems to shrink a few inches in embarrassment.

"Van made the milkshakes without my help," I say. "Give him all the credit."

Carlo shows no signs of having heard me. "I want you two kids to take tomorrow off. Do something fun." He winks.

I think it's the wink that pushes Van over the edge. He rolls his eyes and walks past me to the door.

*

I'm always aware of signs of danger when I leave the restaurant because Jonah, Mayo, and Billy all know where I work. They can find me here after work and force me back to Billy's place or, if I won't go, finish me off anytime they want to.

Van is about the most tuned-in guy I know. So naturally, he notices. "You're watching for those two assholes, am I right?"

"Maybe. It's nothing for you to worry about. If they show up, I'll go with them and leave you out of it."

"Leave me out of what, exactly?"

Well, shit, I can't exactly go there if I want Van to have any respect for me. "It's just business."

"You told me you weren't a drug dealer."

I sigh. "I'm not. Let's drop it, hmm?"

Van starts speedwalking on the sidewalk. Even if he's pissed off, I think I got my way. The subject has been dropped. It takes me a couple of seconds to catch up to him, but I have no explanation for my evasiveness, so we end up walking along the Depot Street sidewalk, side by side, in silence.

By the time we get to the apartment, I can't tolerate the quiet for another second. The thing is, I can't tell him what's up, for too many reasons to count, but I can sum it up easily: I don't want him to think I'm sleazy.

We take turns showering and meet in the living room. Van stands awkwardly beside the couch, and I wonder if he wishes I'd just go to bed and get out of his hair. Speaking of his hair, it looks great, damp and falling over his shoulders. I've never seen a guy with roots as black as coal and white-blond hair. It makes Van stand out.

"You're one of a kind, that's for sure," I say. At first, I'm not sure if I said it or thought it, but his wide eyes and open mouth tell me I spoke the words aloud. It's such a lame thing to say, but I can't take it back. I cross my arms over my chest, wishing I was wearing more than snug black boxer briefs.

Van pulls his white T-shirt down below the waist of his sweatpants. He's kind of tall and skinny, and his shirts drift up a lot. "What's that supposed to mean? You think I'm weird?"

"No...you're just...different."

"I fucking hate that word."

"I mean it in the best way possible, Van." If I'm going to make a move, time is getting short. I've got to do it now. I move so I'm right in front of him, and I put my hands on his shoulders.

They rise almost to his ears and stiffen.

"I've been wanting to do something for a long time."

His eyes widen and his lips twist off to the side. Not a good sign. But still, I lean toward him. Just as I close my eyes and pucker, he pushes me back. "What the fuck do you think you're doing?"

When my eyes pop open, he's staring at me, his gaze icy. "I...I was gonna kiss you."

"Nobody kisses me."

"Is that, like, a law, or something?"

"What if it is, George C?"

"I'm not exactly a rule follower, Van. I'd probably try to kiss you anyway."

As we stare each other down, Van's shoulders gradually relax beneath my hands. And he closes his eyes. If that isn't a "go ahead and plant one on me, dude," I don't know what is.

Van is a few inches taller than me, although he probably weighs almost twenty pounds less. I'm either going to have to stand on my toes or pull his head down so our lips can meet. I opt for the latter. When I put my hands on the back of his head, I'm surprised at how soft his damp hair is. I pull him toward me, and although he's still pretty rigid, he comes. I haven't kissed a record-breaking number of dudes, so I'm not necessarily the best judge, but I'd put money on it: this is a first for him.

I press my lips to his and taste fear mixed with anticipation. But I also taste willingness. What is most evident, though, is his shock. He either can't believe he's doing this or can't believe it isn't half as bad as he feared. Maybe both.

His lips, like his hair, are so much softer than they look. Where at first they're frozen in his usual "I dare you" smirk, they soon mold to mine. When I open my mouth, just a bit, he opens his. And when I turn my head to the side to get the best angle, he does the same. Once our lips are sealed, I sigh into his mouth with satisfaction.

When Van's lips begin to move, I'm the one who's shocked. This kid is starving. He takes over. One hand lands on my waist and squeezes so hard it almost hurts. He then grasps the back of my head, holding me in place. His mouth jerks open and then closes, again and again. No tongue, so I figure that's going to be my job.

I slip my tongue just past his bottom teeth, and he pulls back. It's like he didn't know French kissing is a thing people actually do. His hands fall to his sides, and he utters something that sounds like a drawn-out, "oh," but before I can blink, he's back with a vengeance. When Van grabs my face with both of his hands, chills rise up my spine.

I go with the passion for a few seconds, but then I push back, just long enough to grasp his wrist and pull. "Couch," I say, and am surprised at my breathless tone.

He nods and offers no resistance. Before we move, though, I gaze into his eyes. Mom used to say eyes are the windows to the soul, and she could tell when she looked at mine if I was guilty of some major misdeed. So if Van is freaking out, I should be able to tell by studying him. And Van's eyes are more expressive than anyone else's. I don't know how everybody at work can miss the pain in them. They just believe what Van's *words* tell them—*Stay away from me because my bite is worse than my bark, and my bark is bad!* But *I* see the hurt in his eyes, and I don't plan to make that hurt worse.

Right now, his eyes are as clear as the sky, so the truth should be easy to find. It's evident he's dazed. He's heated up too—there's also no doubt about this. But is he hurt? Scared? Intimidated? I don't think so. All too soon, he closes his eyes and the window to the inside of him is gone.

And then we're sitting side by side on the couch, pressed against each other from our lips to our hips. The kiss continues until we're both gasping, and we have to decide whether it should end here or if we're going to keep on going. It doesn't take much thought on my part.

"We have to stop," I say.

Van nods again, his eyes still closed. "Okay...yeah." His voice is made mostly of breath.

He doesn't ask me why we have to stop. I don't offer that it's clear he's a virgin, and I'm so very much...not. "I should go to bed."

He's exposed—probably more exposed than he's ever been—and I watch as he realizes this. The lips I just finished kissing turn down, and he tugs on his T-shirt and then smooths his hair, all before cracking open his eyes. "I...I'm not gonna stop you, if it's what you're thinking."

The cold dude is back. "Come with me. The bed is way bigger than the couch, and we can sleep together there."

"I don't *do* bedrooms." Van stands and turns his back to me.

"The monster won't be in there. Just me."

"But the monster's always up here." He taps his head.

"Are you sure you won't come with me?" I wish he'd change his mind. I want the heated breath from his starving mouth to breathe on my chest all night. I want his squeezing hands to dig into my side. I'd feel safe. It would be so good.

Van shakes his head vigorously, and I know it's time to leave.

*

The bedsheets are cold. I shiver as I slide between them. The clean, cool cotton soothes my skin, even though I know the warmth I'd have shared with Van would've been better.

Falling asleep has been hard to do since I left home, for lots of reasons. First, I've slept in so many different places since I left home. It's crazy to jolt to alertness every morning with the question, *Where the hell am I today?* And knowing I'm going to wake up this way makes falling asleep tough to do. Second, I've got to be strong all the frigging time. I can't get soft or let my guard down, which is what people generally do in bed when they're trying to drift off to la-la land. And third, at night in bed, I think about what happened with those guys Billy hooked me up with. Well, not so much the details of what happened—I try to block that stuff out. It's way too upsetting to think about. But I obsess over how I felt afterward. Cheap and worthless, even if I wasn't all that cheap. From what I hear—I never saw any money.

The morning after the first time I slept with a dude for money—not that I'd slept much that Friday night—I woke up convinced I was a different person. A person who had crossed a line and could never go back. A desperate man who would do literally *anything* to survive, even if it made him dirty and despicable. The guy who fucked me made Bloody Mary's to celebrate the occasion, I guess, but I asked him to hold the tomato juice in mine. And so I got drunk on vodka. I stayed drunk until late Sunday morning when I stumbled out of the hotel room, sore in mind and body after having been used again and again. Unsurprisingly, the dude who bought my virginity wasn't too ethical to get a nineteen-year-old all boozed up to keep him relaxed enough to...well, you know. Maybe being drunk made it easier for both of us, but it surely helped *me* to endure.

The next time I had sex for pay was the last time. It was with a different dude who happened to be older than my dad. I clamped my teeth together while he did it. *While he did me.* Even as he pushed inside me, I knew that no amount of booze could ever wipe away the memories of slobber on my face and grunting in my ear...and the devastating pain. I decided right there—kneeling on all fours on a motel bed—that I couldn't handle this kind of life for one more day, and I was never going to do it again. I'd eat garbage out of a dumpster in an alley and sleep in the back seat of unlocked cars, but I wasn't going to ever again sell this part of myself.

Billy wasn't pleased with my decision to opt out of our little arrangement, but that's a whole different story. Unfortunately, though, my brain already went far enough into the details of my brief stint as a prostitute to make it hard to get my thoughts under control. I've got to climb onto the horse in my head, break out my imaginary lasso, and try to catch the stray thoughts, so I can put them in a holding pen. Only then I will I be able to relax. But, seriously, thank God for condoms.

"George C?" A stream of light from the opening door cuts through the darkness. "Maybe I changed my mind."

"Hmmm?" I hadn't expected Van to come to me tonight.

"And it's my house; I can sleep wherever I want."

"Of course you can sleep where you like."

"Well then, move over." He approaches the bed. In the beam of light streaming in from the living room, he's pulling off his T-shirt. "You heard me. Move."

I slide to the far side of the bed. He slips in beside me. "Come over here," I whisper, opening my arms to him and having no idea whether he's going to comply or slap me.

Van mumbles, "Whatever." But he snuggles up to me. His chest is slim and smooth, and I like it. His fingers slip through the light tangle on my chest, and he sighs. I think he likes mine too. "Whatever."

We're quiet for a while. Both of us are probably thinking about our own misadventures that have left us alone in life. Loners, even. But loners who are, against all odds, developing a strange, but sort of cool, bond. "What happened to make you hate bedrooms so much, Van?"

He sniffs. "Nothing happened."

"Come on; I wasn't born yesterday. *Something* went down to make you sleep on a couch every night."

"I meant what I said before. Nothing *actually* happened. But a lot *almost* happened."

I nod, as he's told me this before. He's once again confirmed that his loner status is a result of simple fear. "I think I get it."

Van is molded perfectly against me, as his lips had been with mine just a few minutes earlier. "I think…" He stops, swallows deeply. "I think maybe you're starting to."

Saturday

WE WAKE UP clinging to each other. We're like the hugging monkey stuffed animals Mom gave to me for Valentine's Day when I was in the fifth grade and she still considered my naughty behavior cute. Van and I are literally wrapped around each other. I'm sweating a little bit. It's so intense.

Van is still asleep. I wonder what snarky comment he'll make if he wakes to find himself safe in my arms. As I am in his. I slide out from between his arms. I'm not sure if he's ready to deal with this much intimacy so soon after having received his first kiss.

I stand beside the bed and gaze down at him. Van's black and blond hair is spread out all over the single pillow on the double bed. I hadn't missed the pillow at all; I'd been using his shoulder instead. In his sleep, Van smiles this sweet, not-a-smirk kind of smile, and I know what it means when people say something tugs at their heartstrings. At the moment, my heartstrings are pulled tight.

Time to make coffee.

I kneel in front of the coffee maker and slip into the past as I go through the motions of brewing a pot.

"You're up early."

I nearly drop the glass pot to the floor. "Sneak up on me, why don't ya?"

Van flops onto the couch on his belly and closes his eyes. "I will if you insist."

"You've got a wise mouth."

"And you're just noticing this?" He seems so satisfied with himself. I have a strange urge to kiss the smirk right off his lips. "You didn't seem to mind my mouth last night."

I crawl over to the couch and drop onto the floor beside his head. "I forget...I think I need to refresh my memory."

His eyes pop open, but his mouth stays closed. He has no comeback, probably because he wants to kiss me again but doesn't *want* to want it.

"So, Carlo gave us the day off. What do you want to do?"

Van's lips pull into a straight line, and he props his chin in his hands. "Since when are we attached at the hip?" His voice is soft, not his usual challenging tone. I don't think he wants me to answer.

He's not used to having a friend to do things with. I had friends in high school, or at least I called them that. There were always kids around for me to go places with— soccer games, concerts, out for fast food. But mostly to parties. And more parties. And then so many parties they became the biggest part of my life...and being wasted became the biggest part of me. But "parties" is probably the wrong word for what my "friends" and I did together senior year. Parties require music and maybe some pizza and people laughing and talking. We met in my friend Jamie's parents' heated storage unit as often as possible, where we sat on boxes and drank as much booze as we managed to scrape up. Smoked weed when we got our hands on it. Each of us got wasted, night after night, for our own reasons. And we did it mostly in silence.

Plenty of kids party it up in high school, I told myself. But soon, nothing else mattered.

Jamie had too much pressure on him to be the perfect kid—not in ways that would add up to anything meaningful, like getting all A's, but in stupid, useless things. He got punished for leaving a dirty dish in the sink. Or tracking mud on the hallway floor. Daniel's mother was fighting breast cancer all through high school. Our little "parties" gave him a chance to escape intense worry. And then there was Eric, whose reason for living was the fulfillment of a single goal: to be the wildest guy in our grade. Abusing various substances helped him loosen up enough to do this. I wish I'd asked him why it meant so much to him to seem crazy. If I'd taken him seriously, I bet he'd have let me see a different side of him.

You want to know why I spent so much time in high school hiding in a storage unit drinking Eric's dead grandpa's leftover bottles of whiskey, don't you, reader? I should make you figure *this* out too, but I'll tell you plainly that I couldn't accept myself, mainly because I knew my folks wouldn't have been able to accept a son who is, as Dad likes to say, *light in his goddamned loafers.* Even if I always wear high-tops. Drinking until I almost forgot I was gay was easier than coming clean and dealing with the consequences.

The weird thing is, the ending turned out the same. I got kicked out of my house. Dad would have booted me for being gay. He'd said as much, seeing as I'm pretty sure he had his suspicions about me, especially after I went to the junior prom with "a good buddy from another school" who happened to be the dude I was dating. By the time the senior prom rolled around, I had zero interest in doing anything other than drinking in a stuffy storage unit until the world was crooked.

As you can see, I screwed up to the point that Mom and Dad told me not to come back until I grew up. They waited to kick me out until high school graduation last June, which I appreciate. I managed to get my diploma—a minor miracle in itself—but I can't ever go home. People don't grow out of their sexuality. Or their firmly held prejudices.

I'm a gay, homeless adult teenager. I have no family to speak of. I have a low-level fry cook job only because Nikki took pity on me when she found me sleeping on the bench on the sidewalk in front of her apartment building. She worked out the details to get me a job at the diner and took me in for a while. But now I have a friend. Who has given me a home.

"How about we start the day by going down to Lakeland General Hospital?" I ask, fighting the smirk.

Van's hands slide to his hips, even though he's still sitting. "Why on earth would we want to do that, George C?" he asks in the sharp tone I'm familiar with.

"I thought maybe we'd have surgery—you know, to get attached at the hip. It would make the rest of the day so much more challenging. Especially peeing in a narrow stall."

He doesn't want to laugh. I can tell because his lips twitch a little, and he fights it. But then he smiles and snorts. "You're insane."

"Maybe so—because *you're* a freezer pop, according to Walter, and I'm still willing to be surgically joined to you. That spells frostbite."

"How about you pour me a cup of coffee? I'm not awake enough to deal with this shit."

"Okay. Coffee, showers, and then...thrift shops. You need to decorate this place. I'm tired of waking up in what I keep thinking is a department store dressing room."

Van yawns and then snaps, "I'm waiting for my coffee." When did his smile upgrade to a grin?

*

Everything I learn about Van makes me want to know more. For obvious reasons, I hope the feeling isn't mutual. I have no plans to morph into an open book, but I still find him fascinating. And I'm not saying the dude is what you'd call an open book either, but he hasn't made it impossible for me to take a peek under his cover.

Let's start with his clothes. The guy's fashion sense is—how can I phrase this? It's very *autumn*. As in, the fall...when kids make leaf-stuffed dummies with carved pumpkin heads and lean them on the oak tree in their front yards. Today, he's wearing a plaid shirt—black, white, and orange flannel—and worn-out jeans with brown leather boots. His hair is tied in loose braids and topped by a black top hat. Honestly, it wouldn't surprise me if a few crisp, brown leaves fell out of his sleeves. Odd, maybe, but I like what I see. And I'm curious to find out what he'll pick out at the Second Chance Thrift Shop in downtown Leighton.

As we walk to the store from the bus stop, I try to figure out why he keeps his apartment completely plain, when his personal style makes such a powerful statement. I'm not going to lie to you—I have no idea what his quirky, possibly even warped, fashion sense is trying to tell the world—but whatever it is, I'm sure it would be powerful. "And you never decorated your place because...?"

No reply. Just a dirty look. And, yes, it was expected.

"You've been living there for about a year, right?"

Van nods and again gives me the evil eye.

"You've had plenty of time to hang some posters, or maybe throw down a rug, or grab a Yankee Candle or two. Are you short on cash?"

After a third painful glare that practically wilts me, there's a long silence during which I start to wonder if thrift shopping was the right idea for today's fun activity. But he surprises me.

"I refused to put down roots and make the place mine. Partly because I wasn't sure I wanted to stay, but mostly because I wasn't sure Mom and Jake were going to *let me* stay. So I just live there without truly owning it."

His explanation makes sense. "Why are you going along with my idea to decorate the place *now*?"

"Do I have to answer this one?" He tips his top hat so it shades his eyes.

I'm about to say that he doesn't have to do anything he doesn't want to do, when Van shocks me yet again.

"You live there too, now, George C. It's not fair to make you suffer with blank walls."

My eyes fill up with tears in a split second. He's actually pushing back on his fear of getting kicked out of his house to make me happy. "That's cool of you."

He opens the door of Second Chance Thrift Shop for me, and as I walk in, he replies, "Yeah. I'm a supercool kind of guy, but don't get too relaxed. I expect you to help pick stuff out. This is a first for me."

Once we're inside the store, we grab a couple of shopping carts and go our own separate ways. I head for the appliances, as I have something in mind. Van goes in the direction of rugs. It doesn't take long until I find what I'm looking for. I pull it off the shelf and stick it in the cart and go search for Van.

"A toaster?" Van has mastered the fine art of appearing baffled by my idiocrasy. Although I personally consider grabbing a toaster a prime commonsense move.

"Um, yeah."

He's frozen in apparent bewilderment. I'm compelled to explain.

"So we can make toast, you know?"

Van shakes his head fiercely, knocking loose his top hat. He catches it midair and places it in the child's seat of his shopping cart. "That's not a decoration—we're here to get decorations."

"But *toast*, dude...it's kind of a morning essential."

"Whatever." He shrugs. "Come check out this rug I found." I follow him to the back of the store where about ten rugs are rolled up in a row, leaning against a wall. "I like this one...for in front of the living room couch."

He points to a colorful braided rug.

"It's so pretty," I say.

"I figure it'll brighten up the room. You know?"

"Yeah—the walls and the couch are both sort of beige, so this is just what your living room needs. You can stick the coffee table on top of it." It's kind of weird how Van wants such a bright and cheerful rug. He surprises me about every other minute, though. "Let's unroll it and make sure it's not all worn-out."

We drag it out of its place in line and, together, pull it open. Standing on either side, we check it out.

"Looks good to me," I say.

"Like it's never been used," he adds.

"How much is it?"

"Twenty-five bucks. Think that's good?"

I can't believe he's asking for my opinion. It's like the King of Distrust is starting to trust me. "I think it is a fair price." A pang of guilt overwhelms me. I'm the *real* King of Distrust in this relationship, sad to say. Don't judge me.

Van rolls up the rug, and I help him lift it into his cart. "Now, let's grab some art," he says without glancing my way.

We head to the opposite side of the store. It's cluttered with pictures and sculptures and vases and more throw pillows than you can count, stuffed in a giant bin. Van starts to sort through the pictures leaning up against the wall, but I just watch. This isn't my call. It's Van's house; I'm a temporary guest.

After a few minutes, Van stops examining the pictures and looks directly at me. I can't read his expression. "This was your big idea. Aren't you gonna help?"

"It's your house, man. If you want my opinion on something, just ask."

Van folds his arms over his chest. "So you're gonna ditch me soon, huh?"

"Why do you say that?"

"If you planned to stay at my place for the long haul, you'd give a shit what you had to look at on the walls."

"You've got it all wrong, dude. I have no plans on leaving."

"Then get your ass in gear and help me." He goes back to work.

Having been given a specific order, I get to work too. I flip through at least fifty dusty pictures before I find it. "Dude—check this out!" I lift a butterfly migration wall hanging I found in the back of a pile of paintings. The vibrantly painted metal butterflies, clustered together in a circle, are a bit banged up. But even through the thick layer of dust, it's stunning.

"It looks like freedom to me..." His cheeks get bright. I don't think he meant to say his thought out loud. "I like it. It's perfect for the wall opposite the couch." He suddenly seems uncomfortable. "I want to check out bedspreads now." And he's gone.

I place the butterfly art into the cart with the toaster and again try to locate Van.

When I find him, he's holding the edge of a silky purple comforter against his cheek. "What are you gawking at? I'm just making sure it's soft enough."

"Soft enough for what?" I ask.

Van rolls his eyes. "Just rub this against your face and tell me what you think." He shoves the comforter into my arms. I do as he says. "It smells kind of funny, but it's soft."

"I'll wash it in Tide with Febreze." Van snatches it back and stuffs it into his cart, underneath the rug.

We pick up curtains covered with bright yellow smiley faces and a retro Green Lantern poster because Van has a thing for superheroes. And then we head to the cash register to check out.

When I reach for my wallet, Van slaps my hand. "I'll pay." No explanation except for him mumbling something about it being *his* Batcave.

"At least let me buy the toaster," I insist. I'm the one with a fetish for toast.

"If you must," he replies with a loud sigh as I stuff a five-dollar bill into his hand.

"*And* I get to take you out to lunch," I add.

He pretends he doesn't hear and pays the cashier, a lady about my mother's age who smiles when she catches my eye, which seems so wrong. Her nametag says, "Hi. I'm Carol," and she's decorated it with tiny emoji face stickers. If Carol knew more about me, she'd curl her lip at me too.

*

We have to take a taxi home because we have too much to carry on the bus. When we get to his house, we bump into his mother, who is holding a cardboard tray with two cups of coffee in it. "What have you got there, Donovan?"

"Just some stuff." The way Van treats his mother makes me feel awkward, but I know he has his reasons.

"Hey, Mrs. Liss," I say in a bright tone. What? It can't hurt, can it? "Van did a little shopping for his apartment."

"Did he, now?" She peers at me closely. I wonder what she's thinking because she doesn't smile *or* wrinkle her nose in distaste, which would give me a clue as to where I stand.

"Yeah. I think the place is going to look better after we decorate."

"*We?* You mean you and Donovan? *Together?*"

I nod, and her mouth falls open. "My name's George," I offer.

"Sure it is," she replies. "I'm Nancy."

Van blows out a mouthful of air and goes to the sidewalk to get the rainbow rug. I'm left alone to chat with his mother.

"Well, Nancy, I'm just going to help out, you know, with getting his place together."

"How sweet." I see where Van gets his attitude problem. "Don't make noise up there, you hear me, George?"

"We won't." I realize I'm shaking a little. She has the same effect on me as my own mother did. It's like her conviction that, *of course, we're up to no good,* makes anything we do the wrong thing.

Nancy turns on her boot's low heel and walks into the main floor, but she glances back once before she's out of sight. It's almost like she can't believe her antisocial son actually has a friend.

"Don't mind my mother. She's never before seen me in the presence of another human being, and I'm sure she thinks I paid you to hang out with me."

Van's words hit close to home because two men actually *did* pay to be with me. I gulp audibly.

"What? You think letting you stay here for free is *the same* as paying you, huh?"

I shake my head, unable to find my voice.

He storms up the stairs with everything except the rug. I turn, grab the rug by the rope around its middle and drag it to the second floor. When I come inside, Van is sitting on the couch, his head in his hands.

I drop the rug in the doorway and kneel in front of him. "Look, nobody has enough money to pay me to be with them," I tell him, and I mean it. "And if I didn't want to hang out with you, I'd already have found another place to stay."

He doesn't glance up. His shoulder stiffens when I touch it.

"I want to pay rent. It won't be a hell of a lot, but I want to pay you a few bucks every week," I say.

"I don't need money."

I know what Van needs: a friend. Just like I do. But it's the hardest thing in the world for either of us to trust in another person's good nature. "Yeah, but you need to know what we're doing here together isn't about me getting a freebie."

He nods. "If it makes you sleep better, you can stick cash in the coffee can behind the toilet. It's where I keep my emergency fund." Van finally looks up at me. His eyes are a little bit puffy. "I don't give a crap how much you put in there."

"I know." I'm a little bit too caught up in his haunted eyes, so I change the subject. "Let's unroll the rug."

Van surprises me by jumping off the couch. I guess he wants to change the subject as badly as I do. Together we unroll the rug, slide it under the coffee table, and stand beside each other to admire it.

"Let's hang the butterflies now," I suggest.

Van smiles and says, "Maybe we should dust them off first."

After we hang the butterflies on the wall opposite the couch, we're off to the bedroom. "We have to wait to put on the bedspread until I wash it at the laundromat," he tells me. He seems disappointed.

"We can still hang the curtains."

"And the Green Lantern poster," he adds.

"Well, let's get busy."

*

The apartment appears much more colorful and welcoming after we decorate it. So much more like a home. Maybe it's even starting to look like *my* new home. And now we can make peanut butter toast for breakfast. It's the little things that make life worth the effort.

Sitting on the couch, gazing at the butterflies, I ask, "Why did you say the butterfly wall hanging looks like freedom?"

We're sitting so close I can feel him shrug.

"Tell me, Vanny."

"Butterflies can go wherever they want. They don't need the others to take flight."

"But they fly together."

"It's their *choice*, George C."

He's right. The butterflies are all tiny individuals, brushing up against one another, but not forcing themselves on the ones beside them. "Which one are you?"

"Which butterfly?"

"Uh-huh." There's a gray one, semi-hidden in the middle of the rainbow-colored butterflies. I bet he identifies with it, as it's the darkest one.

"I'm the butterfly on the very top...the yellow one is almost alone, but still hanging on."

"I'm the orange one he's hanging onto." I glance at Van, hoping for a smile, but I don't see one. His lips are pulled into a tight straight line. Van seems scared.

*

Although our plan is to go out to lunch, we end up taking a nap on the couch. I relax so much when I'm with Van. And when he leans against me—like now, with his back on my chest and curled up like a lazy cat between my legs— it's as if he's giving me a gift he's never offered to anybody else. He's trusting me. And it means a lot.

I wake up before Van and stay as still as possible so I can soak in the warm comfort for a few more minutes. I need it so much. But still, I wonder how long it would take for him to shove me off the couch if he knew I used to be a prostitute.

The first night with "Mike" was about as close to literal hell as I ever want to get. When Billy dropped me off at the motel and told me "you'd better be good, boy," my urge was to run. But I owed him. He'd taken me in when I was living on the street. He'd let me stay at his place, cleaned me up, fed me. Billy had been *nice* to me. He'd told me I was okay and my parents were assholes for booting their troublemaker, likely gay son out of their home. By the time he asked me for a favor, I owed him one. A big one.

When I arrived that Friday night, Mike was already in the motel room, waiting for me. Room 327, a number I'll never forget. Small talk lasted for five short minutes. We both knew why I was there. And he was what I'd called motivated. We got down to the nitty-gritty in no time at all.

It was horrible. Painful—emotionally and physically. I tried to block it out when it was happening. I'd seen movies about people whose souls split in half during moments like that, and the part of them with awareness floated to the ceiling and watched apathetically from above. But this didn't happen to me. It was pure hell—start to finish—and I was present for every second of it.

After he took my virginity, Mike seemed to relax. And his focus shifted from his pleasure to mine. But I'll swear until the day I die that sucking an orgasm out of me was not about *my* pleasure at all. It was just another humiliation that added to his enjoyment.

Although the original plan had been for me to stay for three hours, he ended up keeping me until Sunday morning. He said I was "that good." All he had to do was make a quick call to Billy, and it was a done deal. There was no need to consult me.

The only time I got to be alone over the weekend was when I went to the bathroom. It was my chance to get away from Mike's roving hands, his slobbering lips, his prying eyes...and worse. Every time I took a piss, I tried to come up with ways to get out of that hellhole. I wondered if my body would fit out the window. I didn't care if I broke my neck when I hit the ground after falling three stories. In fact, hitting the ground seemed like the least of my worries. But I never managed to get the window to open more than three inches. I wished I was still living on the street, in an alley like the one I gazed at from the third-floor bathroom window but couldn't get to.

"We fell asleep." Van's voice is soft, yet I jump at the sound.

Before he can pull away from me, I wrap my arms around his waist and hold him in place. I tell him something my mother used to tell me, back in grade school when she cared. "If we fell asleep in the middle of the day, we must need the rest."

"I guess." He doesn't pull away. "I didn't mean to startle you."

"No worries, dude." I'm glad he doesn't ask me what I'd been thinking about, but I know he hopes for an explanation. I can't take the risk of telling the truth. "Let's go get some food. You must be starving."

"I could eat," he replies, once again haughty. He knows what I'm doing. From personal experience, Van knows exactly what avoidance looks like.

Sunday

THREE CHATTY GIRLS enter the diner.

"I told you he works here, Maria. But you just wouldn't believe me," says a tall blonde girl with a messy bun perched on the very top of her head.

"Donovan Liss is not exactly the type to serve people with a smile. But you were right, okay? I'll give you that much," replies another girl.

The three girls are so strikingly different from one another. One is tall and willowy and blonde. Another is of medium height, a little bit chunky, and has dark skin and hair. The third is tiny with the brightest curly red hair I've ever seen. And more freckles than seems humanly possible.

The tiny red-haired girl walks right up to Carlo, who is working as the host since the usual guy called in sick. "Three for brunch please, sir. And we'd like to request Donovan as our waiter today."

"Of course, dear," Carlo replies. "Is a booth fine?"

"Yes, sir, a booth is perfect."

When Van sees the girls his response is to practically fly into the break room.

"Hey, Jay," I call to the other cook on duty. "Give me two seconds for a quick break."

"You got *one* second, George C. The diner's packed."

I rush to the break room and find Van in front of his locker reapplying lipstick. "Hey, dude. Everything okay?"

"I'm fine."

He's not fine. "You know those girls from school, don't you?"

"Yeah. I know a lot of people who come in here from school; we *are* in Windsor."

That's true. The diner is a popular hangout. Despite his sarcasm, which makes everything that comes out of his mouth seem like the final word on a subject, I sense Van has more to say. I wait for it.

"Those girls are from the literary magazine."

"So they matter to you."

He turns to me and glares like I just killed his puppy.

"I think they came here just to see you."

"Like that would ever happen..."

"Let me know which order is theirs. I'll double the size and make it extra good."

His gaze softens. "You will?"

"Absolutely. Now let's get back out there before Carlo and Jay have simultaneous heart failure."

Van laughs. I love it when he laughs. He doesn't thank me, but brushes me with his shoulder as he passes. It works just as well.

*

I TRY TO catch bits of Van's conversation with the three girls as he takes their order and delivers their food, but it's too noisy in the diner to hear much. He takes his time whenever he stops by their table, and the girls seem to have a lot to say to him.

Before they leave, he comes up to the waist-high wall dividing the restaurant from the kitchen. "George C, they want to meet me for coffee when I'm done with work—to talk about some illustrations they need for Portals." He twists his lips *and* rolls his eyes.

My first response is to wonder why he's telling me this. Then it hits me that he may want me to come along. "You should meet them...and, uh, want some company?"

He nods. "I wouldn't mind if you came with me."

"Then count me in."

"Yeah, sure. I will...if you want to so frigging badly." He smiles for a split second, and it looks so good I memorize it. "Don't have kittens, for Christ's sake."

*

Veronica, Maria, and Mandy, according to Van's nervous introduction, are nothing like the girls I hung out with in high school. Polar opposites would be a better way to describe them. These girls care about their grades, social issues, art and literature, and maybe even about friendship. I highly doubt they have ever gulped down a shot of whiskey or puffed on a joint. But I could be wrong.

We sit together around a small rectangular table at a twenty-four-hour coffee shop called Moon Beans Coffee House, located a few blocks from the Monty-Carlo Diner. The girls have been here since they left the diner earlier this afternoon. There are more messy piles of paper than I care to count, and three open laptops face the three girls. They are hard core when it comes to the literary magazine.

"Tad wants a drawing of a dog. Not a collie, though—he had an orange Pomeranian named Laddie when he was a kid. Well, until it got lost. Or stolen, his family never got to the bottom of it." Today, Maria takes charge of the meeting. "Can you handle that?"

"A Pomeranian is one of those puffy dogs, right?" Van asks.

"Yeah. I'm sure Tad would get you a picture, or you could just google it."

"There was a lady with three Pomeranians in the neighborhood I grew up in... Maybe I can help," I say. I *want* to help, which is weird because I never much cared about stuff like literary magazines in high school.

The three girls gape at me. They're probably wondering why some random kid wants to work on *their* high school literary magazine.

"Do you draw, too?" Amanda asks.

"He does...and he's great." Van replies before I have a chance to slump and shake my head. He usually doesn't lie; my participation in this magazine must be important to him. I wonder why.

"Well, maybe you can draw the Pomeranian for Tad. We also need a picture of a rainbow umbrella, three drawings—or photographs—of beat-up shoes, and an image of a sunset over water," Maria adds. "And we're definitely going to need more. But this is enough to start."

"We want every story to have an illustration or a sketch to go with it—you know, something cool to enhance the writing," Veronica says. "To attract readers."

"We can do that," Van says. *We.*

"What's your name again?" Veronica asks me.

"George."

"George C." Van corrects me about my own name. And I let him.

"Look, George C, the bad news is we're not going to be able to credit you with the images you create. It's a high school magazine, you see?" Veronica's direct, but I'm okay with what she tells me. Truth doesn't suck at all when it's given to you up front. So you can be ready for what happens. "And you don't go to Windsor Academy."

"Not a problem for me," I answer.

"Cool."

I can't believe I'm going to be participating in my first high school, non-sports extracurricular activity at *someone else's* high school, and it's the year after I graduated from my own high school...by the skin of my teeth. I also can't believe how pumped I am for it. I glance at Van, who is sitting beside me. His eyes are wide. I think he's in shock too. He has no clue how I got so wrapped up in his life.

Or maybe it's more that he suddenly has a life.

"Well, the least we can do is buy you boys coffee," Maria suggests. She's grinning and, honestly, seems a little bit guilty. She thinks she's taking advantage of us, but we're all in.

Van starts to say no. "That won't be necess—"

"Sure, thanks," I interrupt. "We'd love some coffee." I'm not about to waste this opportunity to work on the literary magazine. And to have friends who think I'm talented. I like it, even if it's a lie.

Van turns and gawks at me. I casually fake-punch him on his orange-and-black plaid sleeve.

"It's just coffee," I whisper and shrug. "We're not marrying them."

"Fine," he says in a snippy voice and tries to look away before I see his tiny smile.

*

"Where should we go to take pictures of beat-up shoes?" I ask as we settle on the couch to finish the last few pages of *Batman: Hush.*

"Maybe to the Second Chance Thrift Shop again...to their shoe department this time. Those shoes are as worn-out as shoes get."

"Good idea." I'm distracted by his lips. The dark lipstick has worn off, and they are natural and pretty. I want to kiss him again. I want him to keep his eyes open this time so I can see every slight change in his mood. I want to see his fear, his heat, his decision to give himself to me in a way that goes against his every last ounce of better judgment. But I'm worried it will turn into more.

Mike wore a condom when he fucked me, as did the other dude. I don't think I'm diseased or anything. I'm just *less* of a good person than Van. And it's not just knowing I've had sex that messes with my head—it's because I got fucked and paid for it, or Billy did. It's as low and dirty as sex acts go, and it makes me low and dirty too. Van has the right to know about it before things go any further between us, but I can't tell him. I don't think I could handle having him sneer at me—gagging on the inside—at the notion of getting physically close to a guy who sold his body.

I glance across the room and stare at the butterfly sculpture on the wall. At first, I imagined Van was the gray butterfly and I was the orange one, but I was wrong. *I'm* the gray butterfly.

"The book is down there," Van says and points to my lap.

He's noticed I'm staring like a zombie at the wall hanging.

"Yeah, right." I straighten up a little and start to read aloud. Van leans against me. His weight is reassuring.

*

Tonight, Van follows me into the bedroom without a word. No resistance, no explanation, no excuses. I wonder if I've cured him of his fear of bedroom-monsters or if my presence in bed is just a Band-Aid on an open wound. Or maybe it doesn't matter—maybe I'm just glad he's going to be here with me. I have my own share of monsters to fight, and Van's presence makes me stronger.

We strip off our shirts and pants and then hop into bed without hesitation. Van seems as eager as I am to have our chests pressed together. We clamp onto each other and squeeze. Intense relief surges through my veins like adrenaline. It's so right with us.

And he's hard. I'm trying like hell not to be hard, but, shit, I'm a nineteen-year-old dude. It's the most natural thing in the world to want a guy who is fascinating—stylish and smart and artistic. Someone I'm attracted to who keeps me on my toes, especially when we're almost naked and this close in bed. He presses his junk against me and moans. It's the most un-Van-like thing he's ever done. He lets me hear his need and feel his desire as he pushes against me. Now I want to see it.

I place a single kiss on his lips. They're still tight and straight—not yet ready, but definitely willing. I pull back and notice he's closed his eyes. "Keep them open," I say.

"My lips?" he asks.

"Your eyes," I reply.

His eyes pop open. I'm overcome by startling—and also very startled—vivid blue. Van has obeyed my command, and I wonder what other commands he'd obey in this bed. I wonder what it would be like not to be the one who gets fucked. I want to find out what the big deal is about making love to a person who intrigues you. I want it so badly it's a flavor in my mouth. My passion tastes like the sweetest, tartest blueberries picked on the hill behind the house I grew up in.

I kiss him again. The taste of wild berries gushes in my mouth, spilling over my lips. I draw back, hoping to learn if Van tastes the passion too, as it will surely show in his gaze. His eyes are still open. The expression in his eyes is one I'm sure I can't properly describe, but I'm compelled to try. Van's expression is every bit as wild as the flavor of the berries on my lips. He's already lost control; he's dazed. Van can't think right now. All he can do is feel.

"Never...never have I felt this..." His voice is the wind that blows on Blueberry Hill.

"I haven't either," I admit. My voice breaks twice in three words.

"I want things...with you." The way his gaze burns into mine lets me know it's true.

What harm will it do to touch him?

I slip my hand beneath the waistband of his shorts and wrap my fingers around his dick. It's long and thin, and probably beautiful. He falls onto his back and moans again as I move my hand. I lean over him. "Open your eyes," I demand in a tone so powerful it surprises me.

He does, and I see in them exactly what I need to keep going. Trust and desire in perfect proportions. I seal my lips to his but don't open my mouth as I kiss him. He needs to concentrate only on what's going on below his waist, as do I. It doesn't take long.

Van comes in my hand with a shudder and a sigh. The sigh sounds like, "*Now you...*"

"You don't have to do anything to me," I hear myself say.

"Yes, I do. I *have* to," he argues in the voice of the Van I met at the diner. Cold. Aloof.

"I'll do it myself— Just hold me." He has no clue *why* I'd rather do it myself.

Van sighs and whispers, "I'm sorry." He leans up on one arm and gazes down on me. His wild eyes are now feral, like those of the cats I got to know in the alley, before Billy found me.

"Keep your eyes open. I need to be sure..." *I need to be sure you're okay with this, Van.*

Van nods, and I stuff my hand, still damp with Van's come, into my snug shorts. I'm needy for this, and for nothing more. Van's arms come around me, and I'm sure heaven feels this way—not exactly safe and not exactly scary, but very much a place I want to be. I look into harsh blue eyes as I take care of myself. When I come, he smirks.

Monday

I MISS THE hell out of Van when he's at school today. I miss the companionship, mostly. But there's also the blueberry-flavored passion I want to taste again.

Part of me needs to know what's happening with Van and me. Is it friendship? Are we falling in love? I'd cut my tongue out before asking him, though.

The memory of his smirk after I let go last night resurfaces in my brain. I haven't been able to make sense of it yet. Did he smirk because he figured I got what I was after? Or was he genuinely happy that in some way he'd contributed to it? Maybe I'll never know. Maybe I don't want to know.

I pull a few pages out of his sketch pad and go to the doorway at the top of the stairs. I haven't heard movement downstairs at all this morning, so I think it's safe to slip down the stairs and out the front door. Van gave me a copy of the key last week; I lock the upstairs door and then the outside door. I'm not going to risk getting caught going back in later, though. I'll meet up with Van at work.

My phone is one of those crappy disposable ones, so I can't exactly go to Second Chance and take pictures of the shoes on display. What the hell? I'll try to draw a pair of shoes. The picture won't come out like one of Van's, but how can *trying* to sketch a shoe do me any harm? It can't, and so I'm going to do it.

I've never been one to hold back on what my instincts urge me to do, which has gotten me in trouble more than a few times. This time, it should be fine. Sketching shoes is a risk-free proposition.

The lady at the cash register in the front of the store recognizes me, as I do her. "Back for more?" she asks.

"Um…yeah. I guess you could call this round two."

"I have to admit, I had my eye on that butterfly wall hanging for my granddaughter's bedroom."

"Oh, sorry. I hope she's not too disappointed."

"No, she had no idea I was considering buying it. And I'm sure you and your boyfriend are giving it a good home."

I nod instead of shrugging, and then I wave at her. It's a silly gesture when we're hardly two feet away from each other, but she's a nice lady, and I want to be friendly. She's cool with Van being my boyfriend, even if I'm not sure that he is. I wish my own mother would be as cool with it.

The entire shoe department smells a little. I'm sure you know what I mean, so I don't have to describe the scent. The lady's section has lots of pumps—red, royal blue, forest green, but mostly black. I never see women wearing pumps anymore, which is probably why they're all lined up here on shaky wire racks. But I'm drawn to the men's area out of a sense of practicality. I'm going to buy the shoes I plan to draw, and currently, I own only two pairs of shoes—high-top sneakers and my black work boots. A third pair may come in handy, in case of an emergency.

On the shelves are the kind of work boots my friends and I used to call "shit-kickers" in high school, some slightly muddy hiking boots, and more sneakers than you can count. There are motorcycle boots, fancy leather loafers, and preppy boat shoes. I'm drawn to the shit-kickers because they remind me of better days. Or at least simpler ones.

Normally, I'd try to find the pair in the best condition, but today isn't a normal day. I'm searching for shoes I can draw. Old and weathered. Shoes that tell a story but don't smell too badly. And size eleven.

It takes me five minutes to select some well-worn, but not worn-out, work boots. I carry them to the front of the store.

"This is a different sort of purchase than last time, young man," the lady at the cash register says when I put the boots on the counter. When I check out her nametag, I'm reminded her name is Carol.

"It's amazing you can remember what a random guy like me bought."

"I pay attention to the small details," she replies.

Which is exactly what I'm going to do when I draw these boots.

*

It's a cool fall day, the type of day my mom used to call "crisp." Luckily, it's not too crisp to be outside. But maybe I don't have to be. Windsor is an old mill city on the Lange River. The city is gradually being renovated, but there are still plenty of vacant brick buildings I can sneak inside to create my first-ever work of art since probably fifth grade. I tuck the plastic bag holding my new boots under my arm and jog in the direction of the river.

It grows more and more windy as I approach the water. I run past a long row of renovated brick mill buildings—now containing banks and galleries and laboratories—before I come to one that is still vacant and in a state of disrepair. I slip behind it to the side facing the river and find a glassless window low enough to climb inside.

The floor is littered with beer cans, cigarette butts, and empty fast-food bags. There are jagged pieces of broken glass and crumbling bricks everywhere. I find a corner where the bricks on the wall are broken in what I consider to be an artistic manner, and kick the trash out of the way. After I pull the boots out of the bag and the paper and pencil out of my pocket, I sit on the empty plastic bag. Then I arrange the shit-kickers like somebody dropped them in the corner after a hard day at work.

As it turns out, that was the easy part. Leaning over the paper I've placed on the floor in front of the boots, I draw an outline—my gaze on the boots, not on the paper. What I come up with sucks so badly *I'm* embarrassed to look at it, which is saying something since I'm alone. When I try to erase so I can start over, the gravel beneath it shreds the paper. Remembering Van's awesome sketches, I almost give up. I crumple my first attempt and toss it on the floor.

My second try is possibly less successful than my first. I draw the work boots carefully—barely breathing I'm trying so hard—but when I check out the finished product, I come to a sorry conclusion: anyone would think a three-year-old drew it. It soon joins the rest of the litter around me.

I only have one more piece of paper. Accepting this task was a supremely bad idea to begin with since I'm no artist, so I decide to just have some fun with art, like I used to do when I was a kid. I go with a cartoon style—not so real they could jump off the page like Van's images—but you can tell they're work boots. They turn out appearing sort of fun, so I decide to keep going with it. I cover each boot I drew with hearts and peace signs and waves and wings and any other symbol I can think of. When I'm done, they look so crazy I actually laugh. Out loud—and I'm not kidding.

This picture will never make it into a literary magazine, but I had fun and killed some time drawing it.

I fold up the paper and stick it in the bag with the boots and climb back out the window I came in.

Unfortunately, I'm not alone when I step into the alley between the vacant mills. And even more unfortunately, I know the two guys who are blocking my way to the street. Billy's thugs, Mayo and Jonah, are huddled around a smaller dude who's leaning against the wall, and they're involved in an intense discussion. Mayo glances around as I back behind the edge of the building, like he's aware of movement at the other end of the alley. He says, "Shut the fuck up for a second," and they all stop talking.

I shouldn't be as scared as I am right now. These guys can find me at work any time they want. Maybe I just don't want them to find me alone in a back alley. I'm much safer in public. Plus, I don't want them to figure out where I live now. That wouldn't be fair to Van and his family, and I'd have to move because it wouldn't be my safe haven anymore. Their conversation soon starts up again, and I finally can breathe.

I wait behind the building until I can no longer hear their voices, and then I wait an extra five minutes for good measure. When I come out of hiding, I'm frozen to the bone, and all I can think about is taking a hot shower at Van's apartment—my new home. I decide to head back to Van's and sneak in if it seems nobody else is home. I slip out of the alley and onto the street. Mayo and Jonah linger in the distance. I run all the way home.

*

"You got new boots?" Van asks when he returns from school.

"New used boots," I say. "At the Second Chance Thrift Shop."

"Can I check them out?"

"Sure." As I'm still wrapped in a towel from my shower, Van doesn't look directly at me. I think he's trying to respect my privacy. It's a sweet gesture. I go into the bedroom to get dressed.

"Holy shit!" he shouts, and I wonder if a mouse may have climbed into one of my boots in the old mill building and has just made its presence known.

"What's the matter?" I yell back as I pull on black joggers.

"This picture...of the work boots."

I rush out to the living room and snatch the paper from his hand. "I was just messing around when I drew it." I'm humiliated that a talented artist like Van saw my lousy excuse for a drawing.

"It's a damn good drawing."

"It looks nothing like those boots, dude. Admit it."

"Art doesn't have to resemble reality. It just has to say something...or give a feeling. The way you drew these boots is so..." He seems to be searching for the right word to describe my crappy art.

"So...what?"

"Well, it makes me smile."

"Yeah, because you're laughing at it."

Van snatches the picture back and holds it in both hands. And he studies it like it's something serious. "It's like a cartoon, but more than that—maybe sort of like street art."

"Well, I *have* seen stuff like this on the walls of the bus station."

"It's really good. Can I show it to Maria and Veronica on Friday?"

"You've got be kidding me. I was just fooling around when I made it."

He doesn't hear a word I said. "Better yet, come to the meeting with me. You'll make being with those kids more tolerable for me, *and* you can show them this."

A great honor has been bestowed upon me. Van wants my presence at the Portals Literary Magazine meeting. "I guess I could come."

"Don't do me any favors." His words say one thing, but the expression in his eyes is asking me to do him this favor.

Tuesday

I HAVE BIG plans for today. Well, maybe not "big" in the sense that establishing world peace is big, but what I'm going to do is important. Van has done a lot for me. He's given me a place to stay and a little bit of stability in my life. But even more, he's welcoming me into the personal side of his life, when I've refused to do the same. He's confided his fears in me, when I'm sure it would have been far easier to block me out. He's shared his love of graphic novels with me. He's shown me his art and encouraged me to make my own. And he's invited me to take part in the literary magazine meeting with him. Van's giving me some semblance of a life, and I want to thank him.

Before I leave, I stuff the purple comforter from Second Chance and the sheets from Van's bed into a tall kitchen trash bag. I'm so excited about what I have in mind, I forget to be sneaky, and when I reach the bottom of the stairs, I run right into Van's mother.

"Um, hi Nancy," I say and flash a grin, remembering that, every once in a while, a grin worked to lighten up my own mother's mood. I've been told I can be charming when I try.

But not this time. Her glare shrivels my grin, as well as my soul. "What are you doing here, George?" She considers the stuffed trash bag and raises her eyebrows as if she thinks I'm trying to steal something.

"I stayed over last night. And...and I'm on my way out now."

Nancy's shocked. "You stayed *here* with Donovan?"

"Yeah. We're doing an...art project together. It got late so I slept on the couch."

"Try again, George. Van always sleeps on the couch."

I wonder how long Van has been sleeping on couches, but I don't ask.

"What's in the trash bag?"

"A comforter. And some sheets."

"I'm going to need more details, young man." She tosses her fair hair over her shoulder and fixes her eyes— so much like Van's—on my face. "Explain."

"He got a comforter at the thrift store, and it smells a little." I pull silky purple fabric out of the bag to show her. She doesn't choose to take a whiff. "I figured I'd do Van a favor and wash it at the laundromat. And I grabbed his sheets too."

Nancy nods. "Donovan sleeps on the couch."

"Not anymore." I cringe, realizing I may have let the cat out of the bag.

"You and him, huh?"

"I never said that."

"George, I'm not stupid—I can read between the lines." She takes a step toward the door. "And to be honest, I'm glad... I'm glad to learn my son actually has a heart." She opens the door and goes out onto the street.

I'm dumbfounded. I want to yell after her, "Of course he has a heart, but he hides it because of what your perverted boyfriend wanted to do to him when he was a little boy!" But I just stand there and watch her walk away.

*

While the comforter and sheets are in the washing machine at the laundromat, I make my third visit to Second Chance Thrift Shop. Carol waves as I walk past the cash register.

"Hey," I say.

"Back for more?"

"Gonna get something special for a very special guy." I grin like an idiot before I make my way to the back of the store where the home goods are. Without delay, I find what I'm searching for: the huge bin of throw pillows. I take all of them out, one by one, and set them on the floor around the bin to study them. I settle on two shaggy fake fur pillows, one in bright yellow and one in deep purple.

Carol once again proves she has an amazing memory and a mind for details. "Oh, these will certainly compliment the purple comforter."

"They're not for the bedroom, ma'am. I'm going to put them on the couch, in front of the rainbow carpet. To brighten up his place, you know?"

"Well, yes, I do. These pillows will work nicely with that lovely carpet too. And the butterfly wall hanging."

She's so sweet as she rings up the two pillows. I wish Mom had smiled at me the way Carol does, but I guess I didn't give her many reasons.

"Thanks," I say as I reach for the bags.

I head back toward the laundromat. Even though the pillows don't stink, I'll stick them in with the comforter for the very end of the dryer cycle to freshen them up.

I'm roused from my deep thinking by a sense someone's watching me. I glance up and down the street, but aside from a couple of mothers pushing baby carriages and an old man checking his cell phone on a bench, I'm alone.

And clearly somewhat paranoid.

*

"GEORGE C! I'M home!"

I rush from the bedroom, where I've just finished making the bed. I want to see Van's reaction to the new throw pillows on the couch.

He stops short at the entrance to the living room and stares at the couch. I want to see joy. And appreciation, maybe. I'd settle for a mild expression of pleasant surprise. But there's none of that; his mouth straightens into a line, and his eyes go wide. I see nothing to prove, as his mother decided this morning, that the boy in front of me actually has a heart.

"You went shopping today." Van's voice is so cold I shiver.

I come around the couch to stand in front of him, hoping he'll look into my eyes. But he continues to stare at the couch with empty eyes and arms hanging loose at his sides. And in strange opposition, his jaw is clenched tightly. "I did. I went shopping."

I'm skilled at reading body language, as I grew up in a home where I knew by the time I was eleven that I'd never be accepted as I am. I figured out what few things made my mother cover her mouth and smile, and what very much made my father stomp his foot in irritation. I learned when Mom wasn't pleased with me she'd stare straight at me and shoot her displeasure at me in an evil glare before turning away. And when my father confirmed, time and again, that he considered me to be an abomination, he clenched his fists and shook his head. But I don't know how to read the human emptiness before me.

Van brushes past, and I turn to find out what he'll do. He drops onto the couch and picks up the yellow furry throw pillow. He studies it intently as he turns it over, and then over again in his hands. "Why did you do this?"

"Buy throw pillows at the thrift shop?" I ask.

"Yes. Why did you do it?" His tone is accusing, as if I got him throw pillows to hurt him.

"I wanted to bring more color to our...to your home." *To your life.*

Van shakes his head and drops the pillow onto his lap. "You're making it very hard for me, George C."

He's going to ask me to leave. He wants me to leave our home. I lose my breath. *And by giving him a gift, I've made it harder for him to kick me out.*

"You're making it impossible to—"

"To do what?" I can't control my thoughts...or my mouth. I ask a question I don't want an answer to. "Do you want me to move out?"

And finally, he looks at me, his expression still blank. "Do you *want* to move out?"

I don't know what to say. The last thing in the world I want is to leave my beautiful, safe, warm home. The best place I've ever lived. But if Van thinks it's time for me to go, what choice do I have, reader? I've been in this position before, and I left without a good-bye. Some ties are better cut quickly and completely.

"Are these meant to be some kind of payment? Like rent in the form of hairy, eyesore pillows?"

"Why do you think they're payment? Those pillows are a gift. A thank you for what you've done for me, even if they're ugly."

Before I can blink, his eyes fill and tears spill onto his cheeks. "I just can't *do* this with you." Van hops off the couch, and the yellow pillow falls to the floor. He either trips over the pillow or the new rainbow rug, and then falls to his knees, cracks his chin on the coffee table, and staggers to the bedroom. Before he slams the door, he wails, "And I don't even *do* bedrooms!"

I didn't expect such a dramatic reaction to my gift. All I want is to make Van feel good. To feel warm inside...like I've been feeling lately. But I'm still a bumbling idiot when it comes to reading people—in knowing what I should and shouldn't do, and when and how to fit into a home. I walk across the room, pick up the yellow pillow from the floor, and curl around it on the couch.

If Van expects me to move out, I need to pack my stuff into my backpack. And a trash bag—I'll need a trash bag too, because all of my worldly belongings are in the clear plastic bin in his closet. I force myself to stand.

"Time to face the music," I tell myself.

I walk haltingly to his bedroom door, knock once, and then again a bit louder. When there's no response, I open it.

"Van?"

More silence. Maybe he fell into a traumatized sleep. Because I bought him freaking throw pillows.

"If you want me to leave, I've got to pack, and all my stuff is in your closet."

"You washed the comforter." His voice is small.

"Yeah, I did. It smelled funny. Remember?"

"You washed the sheets too." It gets smaller.

"I figured it would be nice for us tonight. You know, when we get home from work— exhausted like we usually are—to slide into clean sheets and..." I go to the closet but just stand here, still and staring. I don't want to open it, because doing that will make the prospect of leaving real.

"I don't want you to go."

I can barely hear him. Still, I catch myself hoping maybe I won't have to open the closet door.

"But you keep doing things..."

My best bet is to wait for what comes next. I stay quiet.

"I haven't shared anything with anybody for so long. And, shit, I'm...fucking scared."

I walk to the bed and stare down at him. He's gazing out the window. "Can I lie down with you?"

Silence.

"*May* I lie down with you?"

A hint of laughter. Just a hint—but it's enough.

"I'm gonna take that as a yes." I climb onto the bed and lay flat. The comforter smells like springtime. Like hope.

"I keep thinking it's not real with us," he says. "Because nobody does shit like buy throw pillows for me."

"Sorry they're so ugly."

"They're the most fucking gorgeous throw pillows I've ever seen."

"Well, I gotta say that's a mighty big change in tune, Vanny." I roll over so I can face him. He does the same. "What did you mean when you said I make it hard for you?"

He answers without even taking a breath, like he doesn't even have to think. "You make it hard for me to be the way I want to be. The way I *have* to be so I can survive."

"I make it hard for you to be cold?"

He nods. "Know why I dress the way I do?"

I don't expect this question. "Sort of like a poor farmer?"

"Yeah."

"Tell me why."

"It's because I want to seem strange, scary even, so the world will look the other way when I walk by. I don't want anybody to think they can get into my life." He rubs his eyes. "And I'm afraid if I tell you any more details about this, it's all you'll see when you look at me."

I know exactly what he means because if I were ever to confide in him about my time as a hooker, I'd be afraid a hooker is what he'd always see in me. "Tell me, Van." Guilt weighs me down like lead in my gut. I'm letting him spill his soul to me—encouraging it even—knowing my lips are going to stay sealed about my own secrets. "Just say it."

"I'm a scarecrow." He tells me and covers his face.

But I'm not surprised by his words. Not at all.

"They scare away all the birds in the field, and I want to scare away all the people in my life. I dress like a scarecrow, and I act stiff and creepy, like every day is Halloween, and it's all on purpose. And it works. Nobody wants to be near me...except for you."

"I'm not easily scared off, you know."

He lowers his hands, softly says, "Boo!" and we both smile.

"I think I know the answer already, but spell it out for me—why do you want to scare off the world?"

Van rolls onto his other side so he doesn't have to interpret my expression when he answers. "Because the world is full of monsters. And since I don't know exactly who is a monster and who isn't, it's safest to assume everybody is. That way, nobody can hurt me."

"Jake made you like this."

"I think so. I got freaked out by how he looked at me...how he *stared* at me. And then he started coming to me in my bedroom, every time Mom worked at night, and I knew he had the power to do whatever he wanted. So, I got meaner and meaner and colder and harder, and then I made myself prickly and creepy and scary...like I said. I'm a scarecrow."

"I want to hold you."

"I don't know why—when you stared at me at work, I figured you had a thing for Halloween."

"Nope. I just have a thing for *you*."

He gasps—just a tiny little gasp. "And now I've told you everything."

I'm quiet because we both know I've told him nothing in return. "*I* just can't..."

"I'll wait for you to be ready to tell me."

I'm never going to be ready to tell him what I've done, but I touch his shoulder, and he turns toward me. "I want to climb into the sheets with you and kiss you until we have to go to work."

"I like that idea."

"Look at me, Van." He does. The trust in his expression is better than anything I've ever seen, and I promise myself to always study his eyes before I kiss him. The room is as dark as it can be in the afternoon, as the shades are drawn tightly, but there are no clouds in his eyes. I pull him against me, press my lips to his, and let my hands explore his chest beneath the flannel shirt. I smile into our kiss when I remember that Van considers himself prickly, because he's so very soft and sweet. It's like I'm invading a sacred space when I push my tongue past his lips. At first, he tightens his mouth, but very soon opens to me. And I find the sweet-tart flavor of passion in his mouth. I can't get enough of it.

We take our time with the kiss. So much time that Van even finds the courage to learn the flavor deep inside *my* mouth. But I want more. I want to taste the rest.

"Let me undress you..." I whisper because I'm almost afraid for him to hear these words.

He nods. "The monster...it's not here today. I think it's gone away."

And just like that, he gives me the permission I need. I sit up and push him onto his back. Soon I'm unbuttoning his shirt and opening it so I can get to his chest. So smooth, like a boy's, but wiry, like a man's, and pale, like the purest snow. I bend almost in half and rub my face on ribs that are easily visible. I'd like to trace each of them with my tongue, but I'm suddenly in a hurry. I push down his jeans and boxers at once. When he helps me get his pants below his butt, I plant a thankful kiss on his belly, just beside his belly button, and there's a tiny giggle I once thought wasn't like Van. I know better now.

"What are you going to do?" he asks, his jeans around his knees and his shirt falling off his shoulders.

I sit back up. "Nothing, if you want me to stop." And I mean it.

"I don't want you to stop."

It's time to find out if the rest of him tastes as incredible as his lips. I lean over and kiss his lips very softly and then trace my tongue over his chin and down his neck. I want to hear him moan, but there's only heavy breathing, passionate and out of control. I think it's *his* breathing, but it could just as easily be mine.

Van touches my hair gently, and I want to do something as sweet and delicate. So I press my lips to his chest—to the place over his heart—and I flatten the side of my face to his chest and listen. Between the heartbeats, he breathes my name. "George C…"

I don't linger on his chest, as Van has started to thrust his hips into the air. And I'm not going to touch his dick with my hand until I've touched it with my lips. I want to shock him with the wet warmth of my mouth.

I think it, and then I do it. I open wide and take his dick into my mouth as far as I can, and then just hold him inside me. He moans.

For a moment, I struggle to block out memories of a much older man taking *me* into his mouth this way—the physical pleasure I felt from the act, with him, was so wrong. I'll never get over how I gave a stranger this part of me. But it will be perfect and special and memorable for Van because I'll make it so.

I move up and down on him, concentrating on the details of his taste and his shape and his smell. When I'm finally still, he pushes into my mouth, and then his hands are again in my hair, toying with each curl. This is making love, and I really think it could heal me. Making love with Van could help me forget how I sold something so precious. As he pushes into my mouth, again and again, I close my eyes, reach into my pants, and grab hold of my dick. I'm ready to come, but I wait until I taste his flavor in my mouth before letting go.

Panting, I fall back onto the bed, but Van has something else on his mind. He reaches down below my T-shirt and pushes clumsily at my pants. He wants to get me off.

"I came right after you did," I say. "I couldn't help it…"

Van sighs deeply and shakes his head, like he's disappointed. "I'm ready to...I'm ready now," is all he says.

I understand his meaning. "Next time." And I force his innocence and my lack of it out of my mind.

He grabs his phone from the bureau and says, "I bought an album on iTunes." And a Journey song comes up.

"Eighties rock." I've always loved the Journey album, *Escape.* Maybe it's because I spent so much time in high school doing just that. Van's done his share of escaping from the world too.

"*My* gift to you, George C."

I place my head on his chest, and we listen to "Don't Stop Believin'" on replay until it's time to get ready for work.

*

Monty is at the diner when we arrive, ten minutes late. For the first time ever. For both of us.

"Nice of you boys to show up to work," he mutters as we rush through the door.

Our excuse is we drifted off to sleep in each other's arms listening to Journey tunes, which we aren't about to actually offer, so we dash into the break room without a word, change our shoes, and grab our aprons.

Walter peaks his head into the doorway and says without a hint of sarcasm, "Liss, today's special is Monty's Mama's Spaghetti and Meatballs." Maybe Walter's noticed Van the freezer pop has started to melt.

"Thanks," Van murmurs with equal sincerity and rushes out to the restaurant floor without applying lipstick.

Walter lingers as I tie my shoes. "You have a good effect on Van. The kid's almost normal now. Well, except for his hair."

"I like his hair," I tell him with a smile. Even though we're late to work, things are pretty good.

Still, I'm nervous walking past Monty to get to the kitchen. He's perched on a stool at the breakfast bar looking like the incredible hulk, but not green. "Hey, George C. Got a second?"

"What's up, Monty?"

"Where are you staying these days? Nikki said you're out of her place."

"I'm staying with Van."

"You and Donovan... How's that working out?"

"Great—it's working out great."

Nikki told Monty and Carlo about my "serious financial struggles" the day after she rescued me from the bench in front of her apartment building, which was a week or so after I left Billy's house. Monty wanted to meet me, and later the same day, I went to the diner for an interview. I was still seriously shaken up by everything that had gone down with Mike and the other dude, and by being threatened to "stick around if I knew what was good for me" by Billy. If I left, he'd explained in painful detail, he had ways of making my life miserable.

I still had a few bruises on my arms and a swollen top lip—not to mention a slightly loose front tooth—left over from my final "discussion" with Billy. Monty noticed and had questions, which I didn't answer honestly since I needed the job so much. But Monty knew I was in trouble. He confided that *Carlo* been in trouble when they met five years ago. Then he told me times *can* change, so I shouldn't worry. I've been working here for almost three weeks now, and it looks like he was right: things are getting better in my life.

Monty is a huge man of few words, but he cares. Carlo is a small man with plenty of words, and he has a huge heart too. I got pretty lucky the day Nikki took me home and brought me to the Monty-Carlo Diner for a job. She helped me get a life.

Work is busy for a Tuesday, and before we know it, the time has come for us to leave. As Van and I walk home, I once again get a strange feeling we're not alone on the vacant street.

Wednesday

VAN LEAVES HIS sketch pad on the coffee table before he goes to school. It's open to a drawing of a rainbow umbrella with droplets of water trickling down each of the different colored panels. Behind it are the most beautiful and realistic clouds that are not actually floating above me in the sky. He did this one in watercolor, and it's amazing—as in, it gives me goose bumps, and I'm not exaggerating. The kids at the literary magazine are going to freak out when they see it.

I figure Van left the sketch pad open to this image so I could check out his art and tell him what I think of it when he comes home from school. It's hard for him to directly ask questions like, "Is my umbrella picture good?" And I get that.

Sitting on the couch with my coffee in one hand, the sketch pad in the other, a sharp knock sounds upon the door. Just one.

I'm not sure what to do.

"I know you're in there, George, so open the door."

It's Nancy. And I've been busted. I put my mug and the sketch pad on the coffee table and tuck my black T-shirt into my camo joggers, as if it will help soften the blow that Nancy's teenage son is living with another guy without her permission on the second floor of her home. Then I go to the door and open it. "Hey, Nancy."

She's standing on the top step with her hands on her hips. "So, you live here now?"

"I, uh, I've been staying here, I guess you could say."

"Aren't you going to invite me in?"

"It's your home. You don't need an invitation." I step back, and she passes me.

In the living room, she stops, her mouth falling open, and stares into the room. It's like déjà vu from yesterday—Van did exactly the same thing as he checked out the new throw pillows. "You guys have done a lot with the place," she says. Admiration is absent from her voice, but then, so is disdain.

"Yeah. We decorated a little bit." She walks over to the couch and drops down on her butt, just the same way Van always does. "How about a cup of coffee, Nancy?"

"Sure. Why the hell not?"

I kneel in front of the coffee maker and fill a mug. "Milk and sugar?" I ask.

"Black," she replies.

When I get to the couch, she is staring at the picture of the rainbow umbrella. "Van painted that," I tell her.

She gasps just the way Van does and picks up the sketch pad instead of reaching for the mug of coffee, so I place it on the coffee table. First, she studies the umbrella, and then she starts leafing through the rest of the pictures. And I let her invade Van's privacy although I want to rip the notebook from her hands. But she's his mother, and

I'm an unwelcome guest. So, like a traitor, I sit beside her, and together, we study the pictures of Van's monsters.

Soon, she comes to the first image of who I suspect, based on her reaction, in some ways resembles her boyfriend, Jake. Nancy's eyes grow round and wet, and her lips twist to the side, exactly as Van's sometimes do. Mother and son are so much alike and yet so very different—it's strange. "Jake..." she whispers, confirming my suspicion.

She proceeds to find another Jake in the notebook, and then another, and in no time, she's crying. This granite rock of a woman is bawling at my side. So, I pull the notebook from her hand and place it on the table beside her untouched cup of coffee.

"I messed up so badly with him." She sniffs. I think she messed up with *both* Jake and Van, but I'm pretty sure she's referring to her son right now. "I refused to listen to him, although deep inside, I believed what he told me."

"Van was scared of Jake...for a very long time. Years, I think."

She nods and wipes her eyes with her wrists. "You're right."

"The fear...it changed him. It made him who he is now."

Again, she nods. "I didn't want what Donovan told me about Jake to be true, so I lied to myself. I convinced myself that my son was jealous of the other man in my life and... Please tell me, what happened? What did Jake do to him?"

"You need to have this conversation with Van, ma'am."

"I suppose you're right. Again." She speaks without conviction, and I doubt the necessary conversation will ever take place. But maybe she understands Van a little better now. Nancy picks up the notebook and flips back to the rainbow umbrella. "Donovan is a talented artist."

"He is. He's on the staff of the high school's literary magazine. As the illustrator."

She gasps again. "Donovan joined a school group?"

"Uh-huh. And they're thrilled to have him." Bragging about Van is awesome. Absorbing her surprise makes it sweeter.

Nancy shakes her head and then stands, never having touched her coffee. "Thank you, George, for letting me in."

I don't think I have to worry about her kicking me out anymore. "It's your house."

"No. This is Donovan's place, not mine." She walks to the door. "And thank you for being here for my son. God knows I haven't been around for him." She opens the door and goes down the stairs.

"You don't have to thank me. Van is awesome. He means a lot to me." I'm all choked up, and I'm not sure why. "You should get to know him too. I think you'd like your son as much as I do."

"Maybe I will," echoes from the base of the stairs.

I'm left wondering whether I've helped Van or betrayed him.

Thursday

JONAH AND MAYO come into the diner tonight. I wish Monty were here. He makes me feel safe, but I have to admit Carlo has proven himself to be a pretty fierce protector too, so I try to relax. And I'm behind the counter in the kitchen, what harm can they cause me back here?

Carlo seats them in Van's section, so he has to wait on them. Lately, Van hasn't been wearing his dark lipstick, and he brushes his hair so it's smooth and silky in his man bun. He doesn't seem intimidating, like when I first met him, and I hate myself for bringing customers like these thugs into the diner, and into Van's life.

Van really isn't worldly at all. His toughness is just an act, and lately, he's let it slide. I'm worried and guilty, and more than anything, I want Jonah and Mayo to leave before they get any ideas about Van. I'm sure Van recognizes them from the last time they came in to harass me. He knows they beat me up, and he's liable to say anything to them. Pissing them off would be bad for his health. My belly twists into a knot.

Finally, Mayo points to me and then to the restroom. I shake my head to tell him, *no, I'm not going to meet you there*. But when he points to Van and makes a throat-slitting gesture, I drop my spatula and practically run to meet him.

Mayo opens the restroom door, and I go inside. He follows me in and locks the door.

"What do you want now?" I ask in an I-don't-care voice.

"What the fuck do you think I want?"

"I'm not going back to Billy. I'm not doing that again."

"I don't see where you have much choice, Curaco."

"And why is that?"

"You fool, we followed you home from the mill the other day. You didn't run fast enough. And we followed you home from here just to make sure. We know where you live."

"So what?" I ask, although I know exactly where this is going.

"We'd hate to have to make trouble for your oddball boyfriend, but, believe me, we will."

I lean over the toilet and everything I ate today comes up in one heave.

"I thought you'd see it our way," Mayo says with a laugh.

"I'm gonna need a few days."

"Well, Billy wants you back on Saturday night—he's got plans for you." Mayo smiles. "If you're still hiding away in your cozy little love nest on Depot Street on Saturday night, we're gonna have a big problem, Georgie. And your skinny boyfriend might get hurt."

"And if I leave town?"

"Billy would rather you stick around and make him some cash. But he can live with it if he never comes across your ass in this town again. You just can't stick around here after taking his kind generosity and then fucking him over by saying no to the agreement you made. It sends a lousy message to his other employees. See what I'm saying?"

"I see." Another surge of barfing overtakes me because I also see what this means for everything I've built in my life—my job, my new home, my relationship with Van.

"It was nice chatting with you. Billy expects you to be waiting for him at his place by three on Saturday afternoon."

*

"You're acting weird tonight, George C." Van's not buying my excuse of having the world's worst headache. "And you've been acting like this since those two assholes came into the restaurant. You haven't looked me in the eye once."

"I told you. I ate something bad. I think I'm just gonna go sleep on the couch."

"No way." He pulls me down beside him on the bed. "We're gonna talk."

I'm shaking my head before I realize it. "I can't, Van. *Please...*"

"I've told you everything about myself! *Fucking everything!*" He's mad. Worried and frustrated, too. I haven't seen him this way before. "You don't fucking trust me!" And he's actually yelling—another first.

I try to get up, but he won't let me. He clings to my arm.

"What are those two assholes holding over you? Do they know something they can use against you?"

"Oh, so you think I killed somebody, and they helped me hide the body?" I smirk. "That's really nice."

"Jesus Christ. I want to help you!"

"Why? Why do you even give a crap?" I'm about to get mean. It's my last line of defense, which I use very rarely. "You don't want anybody in your life, remember? You're a scarecrow—you want to frighten the world away. You don't give a shit about anybody but yourself."

A flash of hurt crosses Van's face, and it pains me. But then Van grabs me by my shoulders. "It's *your* turn to look at *me*." He stares into my eyes, and I do my best to look back, but it's tough because I already know I'm going to deceive him, and he doesn't deserve it. "I know you. And this is not the guy I know." I glance down at the shiny purple bedspread, but Van shakes me just hard enough so I'll look back up. "I've never told..." He clears his throat and starts over with a shaky voice. "I don't say shit like this to anybody. But I'm telling you now—I care about you. A hell of a lot."

I love you too. But I have to leave soon.

Suddenly, he changes his approach. He relaxes his grip on my shoulder and leans forward so his lips are just beneath my right ear. "You can trust me," he whispers. "And I'm not going to let you sleep alone tonight." With those words, he grabs the bottom of my T-shirt and pulls it over my head. "You're so beautiful." He pushes me back on the bed and goes to work on my pants. In a second, they're unzipped and unbuttoned and sliding down my legs.

"Stop...you don't want to do this." I protest for a million reasons, but he doesn't stop.

Next thing I know, my briefs are being tugged off my ankles.

"I've...done things. Sexual things." It's the best I can do in terms of a confession.

"Of course, you have. That's why I got condoms." He pulls one out of his pocket.

"We can't have sex. I'm not...like...ready." I tap my head as I lie. Then I touch my heart. The truth is I'm so incredibly ready to make love to Van, but he doesn't know about Mike and the other guy. About how I sold myself to pay a debt.

"That's fine too." He stands and pulls off his clothes. "We can do more of the stuff we've already done. I don't need sex."

Van climbs on top of me and covers me with his body. I'm warm and safe.

"Is this all right?"

"It's so good." It's perfect—like I'm in heaven. But it's hard to enjoy, knowing hell is right around the corner.

Reaching between us, he lines up our dicks. "I'm gonna rub us together, okay?"

I nod once, still distracted by my fear of the future.

"And while I'm doing that, I'm going to kiss you...and prove beyond a shadow of a doubt that you can trust me."

"I want to trust you but...it's just that..."

His lips come down over mine before I can finish my excuse. And I let myself go. I slip into the pleasure and the safety and the wonder of this last time I will sleep all night in what I've come to think of as *our* bed. With Van, who has become my best friend and my lover and my family, wrapped up in one unique package.

I grab onto his butt as he grinds his hips against mine. It's impossible to think, to worry, to remember I have to leave him, because he's kissing me in a way I've only seen in the movies, passionate and needy. My pleasure is growing by the second.

"I can't wait too much longer..." Van says what I'm thinking into my mouth, and I utter a sound that means, *me too.*

Then we're coming, and maybe this isn't sex, but there's no doubt we're making love.

I love you. I'm so sorry about what I have to do.

Friday

"MEET ME AT the entrance to Windsor Academy at 2:45 p.m. I'll sign you in, and we can go to the Portals meeting together," Van says as he fills his messenger bag with notebooks and sketches.

I'm in a purposeful daze. It's either that or cry my ass off, and I can't exactly start bawling until after Van leaves for school. Nothing like giving up all my secrets—he'd know something's seriously wrong. This is so much harder than when I left home last summer. "I'll be there."

"Bring the drawing of the boots."

"I will."

Van slings his messenger bag over his shoulder and heads for the door, but he hesitates at the doorway to study me one more time. "And we're going to talk this weekend. I mean it." His eyes are so clear this morning—bright blue and hopeful about the future. In this way, he's a different person than the guy I met a few short weeks ago. Different, but still slightly wary. Van has a second sense for when he's about to be screwed by life.

"On Saturday, we'll talk," I lie, glancing away.

"Carlo gave us the day off again, so if it's warm enough outside, we can go to the Lange River. We'll drink coffee and talk about everything there."

I find myself being drawn by an unknown gravitational force to his side. He leans in for a hug, and I dig my fingers into his shoulder. It used to be the other way around—his fingers would cling painfully when he held me. Everything is different now.

"There's nothing you could tell me that would change how I feel about you."

"I know." I'm starting to believe him, but it's no longer the point. I have to leave town to protect him. "I'll see you this afternoon."

As soon as Van leaves, I get to work. I toss my clothes into a kitchen trash bag and take them downstairs. Once I'm outside, I hide the bag in the alley between the duplexes. Then, I put the rest of my stuff into my backpack and stick it inside the bin in the closet.

Next, I set about cleaning his place like it has never been cleaned before. The least I can do is leave him with a sparkling clean apartment. It's a very minor way to thank Van for everything he's done for a dirty dude like me.

It takes me several hours to get it so clean it wouldn't hurt to eat off the floor. And then I allow myself an hour to cry into the furry purple pillow on the couch before getting in the shower.

I really love this home. I really love Van.

*

The only activities I did in high school were sports. I was a decent soccer player and downhill skier, but by the time junior year rolled around, all I did outside of school was party. I never even considered joining Yearbook Staff or Amnesty International, let alone the school literary magazine. In fact, I don't even know if my high school *had* a literary magazine because I wasn't tuned in to things like that. And here I am at Windsor Academy's Portals Literary Magazine staff meeting. With my own personal art project to offer them.

We're all clustered around a long table in the back of the room, our art spread out for all of the group members to view.

"The short story that will go with the boots you drew is called 'Walk a Mile in My Shoes.' It's about a boy who wakes up every morning to find a different pair of shoes beside his bed. He puts them on and is magically transported into the life of the pair of shoe's owners."

The guy speaking, Alex, is as skinny as a beanpole and has the world's most enormous mass of frizzy black hair. It defies gravity by standing straight up off his head. His glasses aren't small either. "I need two more pictures, at least, of shoes drawn in this same style—I really like it, George C. It's modern and fun and will draw readers to the story."

My heart is pounding. *He likes my shoe picture.*

"Think you can draw more shoes, maybe one pair for a dancer and a pair a businessperson might wear?" Maria asks.

I *could* do it if I was going to be around. But I won't be. "I probably can," I lie. I just can't bring myself to say no. Plus, if I told them I can't do it, Van would ask questions I can't afford to answer.

A tall, preppy kid points to the charcoal sketch of a dog. "About the Pomeranian, Van, it looks almost exactly like my dog, Laddie. It'd be perfect if he had a little bit shorter nose and slightly bigger eyes."

"I can do that, Tad. No problem," Van assures him, somehow managing to sound like he cares a lot and doesn't care one bit at the same time.

"Thanks, man." Tad is clearly pleased. "And, uh, great job."

"I think the last thing we need is a picture of a family, right Mandy?" Maria asks, and we all glance at the tiny ginger girl.

"Yeah. I'm working on a poem called "Quality Time." I think a picture of a family doing something fun together would be perfect."

"Doing what?" Van asks, completely clueless. I'm pretty sure he hasn't spent quality time with his mother in ages. Not that I'm an expert on fun family activities.

"You know," Maria says, "fun stuff families do together. Riding bikes, eating ice cream, bowling— whatever."

Van nods, but he seems distracted. "Sure."

The group has already drooled over the watercolor umbrella and sunset Van worked on last week and are soon busy talking about how they want the back cover of the booklet to appear. I glance at Van, who is in the middle of the group. He's animated as he tells them his idea for a spiral cobblestone path circling the school on the front cover and leading to the back cover and then off the page, suggesting that the reader is heading off to new reading adventures.

New adventures. This puts a positive spin on what my disaster of a life will be filled with starting tomorrow.

The next thing I'm aware of is Veronica adjourning the meeting. "I think this has been an incredibly productive session. I'll see you all next Friday."

I grab my coat as Veronica and Maria gather the art and the articles for the magazine. When I glance at Van, I catch him studying me.

"Let's call in sick to work tonight and grab some Thai food and talk at my place instead of waiting until tomorrow," he suggests.

Van hasn't missed my odd behavior. It's hard to believe he can read my signs so easily. Not too long ago we were strangers. "We can't leave Carlo high and dry. It's Friday, and it'll be busy tonight—he needs us," I reply. Talking is not an option. My only option is leaving.

I walk past him out the classroom door and into the hallway. He follows without another word. We head straight to work.

*

It takes a long time for Van to fall asleep tonight. At first, I worry I'll fall asleep while I'm waiting for him to doze off and lose my chance to escape into the night. But when I pull his head onto my chest and brush my fingers through his black-and-blond hair, he finally relaxes and drifts away. I wait an hour more, until his breathing is heavy and steady with deep sleep, and then I slide him off my chest and onto the sheets. And I slip out of bed.

It's pretty easy to sneak out from this point—at least it's easy in a physical sense. I grab my backpack from the bin in the closet, leave the bedroom on tiptoes, and collect my sweatshirt from the back of the couch. Once I slip my feet into my high-tops, all I have to do is walk out the door. But I hesitate at the doorway to the stairs and soon find myself once again sitting on the couch with Van's sketch pad in my hand. On a fresh sheet, I write the only words I can think of. *I'll leave the key to the front door under the doormat. And Van—I'm sorry. I couldn't stay.*

I write a few more words letting him know there's no use trying to find me.

And then I'm gone.

Part Three: Donovan

Saturday

WHEN I WAKE up, George C isn't beside me in bed. And I don't smell coffee brewing, which is strange. Usually, the first thing he does when he wakes up is make a pot of coffee. I drag my ass out of bed and into the living room. There's no sign of him there either. I shrug and head for the bathroom to take a quick piss.

As I put on a pot of coffee, it hits me that I haven't done this since George C moved in. It's messed up how a new person in your life can so completely change your habits. As the coffee brews, I sit on the couch and notice something I missed yesterday: my apartment has never been cleaner. Not even when I moved in. It smells like pine, and there isn't a speck of dust anywhere. George C must have cleaned the place when I was at work. He's a sweetheart, and I'm damned lucky I met him.

I have no clue where he went this morning, though. He's never been gone when I woke up before. He was probably in the mood for doughnuts instead of toast and took a walk to find us some. I pour a cup of coffee and decide to start work on a picture of a garden Maria needs for Portals.

I grab a pencil and flip to the next clean page of my sketch pad. And there's a note in George C's handwriting. I swallow hard because this can't be fucking good.

I'll leave the key to the front door under the doormat. And Van—I'm sorry. I couldn't stay. Don't bother trying to call me. I dumped my cell phone.

"What the fuck is this?" I ask aloud. Of course, nobody answers because I'm alone.

I've been dumped on my ass.

George C is gone.

*

The first thing I do when it sinks in that my new roommate took off on me is to check the money can in the bathroom. I need to be sure that what we had together wasn't only about him robbing me of my emergency fund. As I storm into the bathroom, it hits me that stealing is a very cynical thing for me to suspect George C of doing. But the truth is, I *want* the can to be empty. If he's stolen all my money, then I can be pissed off at him. I can hate him. And hatred is so much easier to deal with than abandonment.

I dump out the cash can on the bathroom rug. It's all there and then some. George C paid me well for his short stay in my home. Next, I collapse on the spotlessly clean bathroom floor. My shock is intense. The betrayal is worse. He left me without warning. He ditched me knowing how much I need him. He lied to me when he said we'd talk over his problems on Saturday.

I jump to my feet and rush to the bedroom on a sudden impulse—an urgent need to convince myself this is really happening. I throw open the closet door and find an empty bin.

George C is gone. He left me. And even if he didn't rob me blind, I fucking hate him.

I can't look at the damned bed because it makes me think of George C. It screams his name, and I can't hear that right now. I run to the living room and jump onto the couch, kick the hairy yellow and purple payment-pillows across the room, and then I fall onto the couch on my face. But I refuse to cry. There's nothing new about this: he's merely the *next* person in my sorry life to betray me. He's certainly not the first, but he'll sure as shit be the last, because I'm never going to be such a fucking fool again.

Fuck George C. Just fuck him.

*

I wake up for the second time today at noon. I'm not hungry. I'm not thirsty. And I wish like hell my heart could be as numb. But it can't. My fucking heart is broken.

There it is—*I said it*. Yup, reader, it's true. Donovan Liss possesses a heart. And he let the wall around it down, and it got pummeled. Chewed up. Spit out. Are you happy? Do you think the lying little bitch got what he deserved?

Well, I'm not going to let it be that way for me again. And I'm not going to just lie here and fall apart. I have to do something. I have to stop thinking George C had given me life and, instead, focus on how he'd truly robbed me of what little life I had.

I shower with haste and throw on clothes that would better suit a leaf-stuffed-dummy on somebody's rickety front steps than a teenage boy. And you know what? I'd been considering replacing some of my scarecrow attire with everyday, average human being clothes. Don't get me wrong, I wasn't going to head off to shop at Abercrombie & Fitch. I decided I'd stop by the Second Chance Thrift Shop to pick up some solid-colored button-down shirts, maybe a golf shirt or two—nothing too preppy—and a couple pairs of pants that aren't made of worn denim. Fuck, I'd even had my eye on George C's joggers—I figured I'd look decent in them if I could find a pair in extra-long. But the plans for my normalizing makeover are history because the human being who made those plans is dead.

And in his place is the scarecrow, more stiff and rigid than he was before. Unlike the flimsy one on *The Wizard of Oz* who was worried about not having a brain, *this* scarecrow has the tin man's problem: he's now heartless. But unlike the tin man, he doesn't give a shit.

I throw open my apartment door and leave without locking it behind me, having no further need of privacy. I stumble down the stairs.

And so the scarecrow lives on...a primitive watchman, alone in a field, ready to fend off the hungry birds while suffering any kind of weather. Maybe today I'll bake in the sun. Or maybe wind-driven rain will shoot me like pellets from a gun. It's all the same to me.

I've got to be numb. To feel nothing.

I'm heartless now.

Hollow eyes and sunken cheeks and a stitched-up mouth that will never speak a sweet word again. Stiff wooden arms stick out straight from my sides. But I don't suffer for the survival of all humanity; I suffer only for my own survival. And I have no need of lower limbs. The bottom half of my body is a crude wooden post, draped in a worn pair of cast-off jeans. What use has a scarecrow of legs to jump for joy with or a dick for making love?

Here I am: the farmer has dragged me to the center of the cornfield where he propped me upright and abandoned me to random weather and tortured thoughts. I like it here, all alone.

I'm jolted out of the cornfield in my head when I bump into the last person in the world I want to see. And maybe you think the very last person I'd choose to see is the man who made me so untouchable and isolated from the world. But it's my mother—who is lower than Jake on the totem pole of my life's betrayal. She didn't protect me. She instead chose to preserve her warped relationship. And the woman clutches a plate of blueberry muffins and is heading up the stairs. Wearing a goddamned smile. What the fuck is this?

"Donovan," she says, surprised to see me.

"Where are you going with...with muffins?"

"I thought..." Mom stops speaking to clear her throat and then begins again. "I thought you and George would enjoy some homemade blueberry muffins...uh, on a Saturday morning." Her face is a satisfying shade of humiliation-magenta.

"Who are you and what did you do with my mother?" I ask.

"George is a very nice boy."

I can't find words. My mouth falls open, and my stare shifts from her red face to the blueberry muffins, and back.

"George and I had a little chat. He told me he cares for you."

My chin drops even further. And then I get my act together and spit out, "Well, he's gone."

"He left you?"

"Doesn't everyone?" I ask and expect her to accuse me of driving that "very nice boy" away with my utter wickedness.

"I'm sorry, Donovan."

Admit it, reader: this remark is surprising.

"Don't be. It doesn't matter."

"Eat dinner with me tonight...son."

Again, I'm speechless. My chin drops two inches, at a minimum.

"Jake left too."

"He dumped you?" I fight the urge to chuckle. "Welcome to the Liss Family Losers in Love Club, Mom."

Again, she clears her throat. And it hits me that we've been staring at each other. My suffering gaze has been connected to hers, sporadically at least, since we bumped into each other on the bottom step.

"No, I asked him to leave." She's shaking all over. Even her chin is trembling. "Like I should have done years ago."

"What the fuck?"

"I believed you then. I knew you were telling me the truth...and I...I screwed up, Donovan." I take the plate from her hands as I'm afraid she is going to drop it, and the last thing I need is a mess to clean up on these stairs. "I'm sorry."

I squat down and place the plate of muffins on the stairs. "And you think baking me muffins is going to fix it?"

She shakes her head.

"It's too late. I hate you, Mom."

Mom covers her face with her trembling hands, but she manages to whisper, "Dinner's at five."

The scarecrow leaves the building.

*

I walk aimlessly along Depot Street in a new sort of trance. A trance in which I'm consumed with a monster named George C...who turned into an angel only to morph back into a monster again. And rip me to pieces.

There's nowhere safe for me to struggle through this daze. I can't go to the Thai restaurant for lunch—even the scent would undo me. Bookstores bring back painful memories, too, because George C and I bonded over graphic novels. Even *thinking* about the couch in my living room guts me.

Somewhere along the line, I lost the ability to wear my isolation like a badge. Alone feels fucking lonely today. In a few short weeks, I melted into a puddle of tender emotion. But I'm certain I can get my apathy back. I'll find it again if it's the last thing I do. I'll scrape it out of the folds of my scarecrow clothes with my fingernails if I have to. But I'll find it again.

I felt little pain before I met George C. Sure, there was plenty of denied longing for what I wished could have been—a family life with Mom, involvement at school, friends at work. But the bitter pain of my mother's betrayal was long gone. I hadn't suffered with it since I was fifteen years old, or so, when I knew for certain Mom had chosen Jake.

In my trance, I wander the city streets for hours without a sense of where I'm going, and all the while, trying not to dwell on the monster named George C who haunts me. Trying like hell not to wonder if a person can fall in love in two weeks. In two days. In two hours. In the two minutes after I first saw him at the Monty-Carlo Diner, as he stared at me like he alone saw the truth inside the scarecrow. Because I think maybe I did, fall for him— in two quick seconds.

"Young man!"

I'm dragged from my trance by the shrill sound of a woman's voice.

"Sonny-boy!"

I swat at the hand that grips my arm, the fingernails that press into my flesh and—

"Young man, please come into the store! I have something for you!"

I'm standing in front of the Second Chance Thrift Shop. *How did I get here?*

"He told me you'd come here this morning and that I'm to give you a gift and a message." I recognize the lady. Petite and African American and a little bit nosey.

"What do you want, lady?" What on God's green earth is she babbling about?

"I'm Carol. And this is not about what *I* want, it's what your young friend, George wants." She grabs my arm again. "Now come into the store."

I'm so stunned I obey.

I follow her to the cash register where she reaches under the counter and pulls out a sketch pad. "Your friend was waiting here when the store opened this morning. He gave me this and told me you'd come in today, and when you do, I should give it to you." Carol extends the sketch pad to me. A sharpened pencil is taped to the top.

"George C came here? This morning?" I ask before I take it. And before I remember I don't give a shit. "Was he okay?"

"Honestly, son, he didn't seem like his usual friendly self. He was nervous, or maybe afraid. I asked him what was wrong, but he didn't answer me. He left in a hurry."

I swallow deeply. It makes a loud gulping sound that should embarrass me but doesn't. And I should refuse to take the notebook because I hate George C. But I'm not that strong. "Thank you, Carol."

I grasp the notebook and am out the door in an eager sprint.

*

I walk for another hour, debating my human need. What is best for me—and by this, I mean, what is the safest direction in which to go to protect my fragile heart? Because, yes, this scarecrow actually does have a heart, and, yes, it *is* fragile. It broke so easily after years and years of preparation to be tough and cold and hard and prickly.

I find myself on a park bench overlooking the Lange River. Near the Local Fine Art Museum of Windsor where George C convinced me I have what it takes to create good enough art for Portals Literary Magazine. Where he made me believe I can draw more than just monsters.

The grass around me is somehow still green; it clings to the last remnants of fall, although winter is just around the corner. I glance toward the river. It's a windy day, and a father with two kids scrambling around him is flying a single kite—fluorescent orange in contrast with the blue sky. They're all laughing and shouting and having fun in a way I never could—not even as a child. Maybe I was a scarecrow, even back then.

I identify with the neon-orange kite flying high in the sky—dipping and swirling and twisting in the wind. Like me, quite conspicuous to anyone who looks its way, yet very much alone. I start to pull in a breath, but a gust steals it away, and I gasp. And then I smile because I enjoy the tiny moments of drama I create. *It's safe to gasp when I'm the one responsible for the distress behind it*, I tell myself and try like hell to believe it.

And then I open the cover of the notebook. Gazing up is a drawing of me. It's in the same cartoon style as the work boot George C drew, but, somehow, this image is more realistic. He captured the thing about me that makes me…me. The first things I notice are my eyes. My suffering eyes…perfectly round and wary. Hyperalert, almost like I'm ready to scramble off the page at a moment's notice. George C knows my eyes are as blue as the sky on a sunny day like today, but he drew them to seem dark. Surrounded by shadows. And huge. I wonder if this is how he sees my eyes. I wonder what went through his mind when he gazed into eyes so troubled.

My nose is but a single curved line and my lips, which notably aren't black, are hardly there—narrow and undefined. The most notable thing about them is the smirk they wear. I didn't realize I smirked so much that George C would see me this way in his mind's eye, but there's a tiny dimple—plain as day—to which my lips are pulled. The top of my head where the roots are black isn't part of the sketch. It's as if my unnaturally dark roots never sent much of a warning message to him at all. White-blond hair hangs all around my face, wild and unruly.

The image is disturbing. I wonder if I seemed so arrogant and untouchable to him. And at the same time so terrified. This cartoon, unlike the boots he drew, doesn't make me smile. I don't even smirk.

I turn the page and there's a note from George C—the second one of the day. I want to read it more than anything in the world, and at the same time, I want to rip it out of the notebook, tear it up into the shreds he tore my heart into, and scream as I throw it in the wind like it's as insignificant as confetti at a rock concert. And watch as the tiny scraps ride the gusts swirling over the choppy Lange River until they're far away from here.

For a moment, I'm frozen, as it's too difficult to decide if I care enough to read the note. No— that's not it all—and you, reader, of all people, know I'm trying to put a positive spin on the conflict I'm dealing with. Deciding whether or not to invest my broken heart enough to read the words George put down on paper is far less about raw pain and much more a purposeful choice. You know as well as I how much I'm struggling to admit I still care about yet another person who ditched me for something better.

Does it matter why George C is gone? Can anything he says in a hastily scribbled note soften the blow of waking up alone when I truly believed he'd always be there for me?

I don't think so. But I read the note anyway.

Van—

You think I'm just like your mother and have decided my life will be better somewhere else with someone other than you. But it isn't that way at all.

I hid so much from you. Not everything—I didn't hide who I am and how I view the world and how I feel about you—but still, I hid a lot. And now that I'm gone and won't have to see your eyes filled with disgust when you look at me, I'll tell you what I worked so hard to hide.

My parents kicked me out after high school graduation. In their defense, I was a disaster of a son—I partied way too much. And worse—in their opinion—is that I'm gay. To them, both sins are unforgivable. And so I moved here and tried to build a life, but I couldn't make ends meet. I landed on the street.

This guy named Billy found me there. He saved me, or so I thought. He took me in and cared for me. I owed him my life. And I paid my debt—or, I paid some of it.

Billy arranged for me to sell something that should never be sold, and it wasn't drugs. Here's the sickening truth: I had sex with men for money. I was a prostitute for an awful and shameful five days of my life.

The men used protection; so disease isn't a huge worry. But still, I feel dirty.

I ran from the arrangement I made with Billy, which is unforgivable to a criminal like him. It's why Jonah and Mayo—the two thugs who came into the restaurant a few times—were after me. They tried to convince me to go back to work for Billy, and I refused, even after they beat me up. But Van, when they found out where you lived, my only choice was to go. They've agreed to leave you alone if I get out of town. So it's either move out of the area or go back to working for Billy. I can't do that.

I'm sorry I dragged you into my mess. But please don't let my mistakes push you back into hiding. Your life is opening up to better things. I watched it happen—and it was awesome. You don't have to be a scarecrow anymore.

You owe me nothing—it's the other way around— but still, I have a favor to ask. Would you tell Monty and Carlo why I can't work at the diner anymore? And please thank them for helping me out and giving me a job I liked and was good at.

Van—you were the best friend I ever had. I hoped we could be a lot more. I think we were on our way to that too. And since I'm coming clean, I'll tell you the rest—I fell for you. I wanted to stay in our home and in your arms forever.

I hope you can forgive me.

George C

I close the notebook and hop off the bench like it's burning my ass. There's so much information swirling in my brain I almost can't make sense of—and I need to move so I don't break down. If I start to cry, I'm not sure I'll ever stop.

I walk, but soon find myself running, in the direction of home. It's cold outside today, and I wonder how George C will stay warm. I never even saw a winter coat in his bin in my bedroom closet. As I run, I search the streets and sidewalks and alleys for a boy with rock 'n' roll hair and puppy dog eyes. But he's nowhere to be seen.

My anger doesn't vanish, even with a rational explanation. My pain doesn't magically disappear either. But the rejection—the sense of abandonment—is gone. George C did what he had to do, and he did it mostly to protect me. This is nothing like my mother's decision to listen to her lover's weak defense rather than her son's honest accusation. To push me out of her life in order to pull Jake in, because she couldn't have us both. Yeah, reader, this situation is different.

I'm equally powerless, though. I have no clue where George C went. I can't find him and tell him I don't give a shit what he did with his body. My only concern is what he did with his heart. And he *told* me: he fell for me. *That's* what he did with his heart.

Once I get home, I storm up the stairs as a new idea emerges.

I throw open the door and go straight to the couch, stopping only to pick up the furry purple and yellow throw pillows from the floor where I kicked them this morning. Carefully, I arrange them on the center of the couch, and then I drop my ass between them. After turning past the two pages of the notebook George used, I pull the pencil off the top and draw.

I'm not certain if I was in a trance or merely absorbed in my art, but an hour later, George C is on the page before me. The last time I drew him—the portrait I think of as Monster-George—I drew a very close likeness to his actual face. It was lifelike. It was real. But this time, I created a work of art. On the paper is the George I see with my heart, not just with my eyes.

This image is striking. His long layers of brown curls beg to be touched by *my* fingers. His dark eyes are every bit as "suffering" as mine, but much more sweetly so. He glances off to the side, though, rather than directly at me, hiding what he considers to be an unforgivable sin, but that I know it was merely what he had to do to survive. George C's nose is straight, but his nostrils flare with the passion *I* bring. His parted lips are deeply colored, even bruised, from *my* hungry kisses. This is the George C of my bedroom—of *our* bedroom. He's exotic and sensual and is made for me.

I want him back.

And so I turn the page and write two words.

Come home.

Then I slam the notebook shut and leap from the couch. I run right back out the door, down the stairs, and onto the street. This time, I know where I'm going.

Reader, I can make this right. I can make us safe. I can fix everything that went wrong.

*

I barge through the front door of the Second Chance Thrift Shop.

"Carol! Has he been back?" I shout my question before I consider that we're not alone in the store.

She turns her attention from her customer and says to me, "Give me a second to finish here, dear."

I lean one elbow on the end of the counter to endure the longest second in my entire goddamned life. When the customer leaves, Carol comes out from behind the cash register and stands before me.

"Has George C been back here? Have you seen him?" I ask again, breathless. Then I straighten and grip her shoulders. I don't attempt to shake an answer out of her, although it crosses my mind.

"I'm not sure," she replies and glances out the huge side window.

"What the fuck is that supposed to mean? Was he here or not?" I drop my hands to my sides and run to the window. I search in both directions. Sidewalk and cars passing by on the street, and nothing more.

"Just what I said. I have a feeling he's around the store, but I haven't actually seen him."

"Okay." I pull in a deep breath in an attempt to calm myself. It only sort of works. "I'm sorry for getting so worked up. It's just…"

Carol pulls the notebook out of my hand. She opens it and turns to the drawing of George C. "You don't have to explain being in love to me, son. I've been there; I understand it."

Heat races up my neck and spreads across my cheeks. Carol is certainly bold, but she's also correct. "If he comes back, will you give it to him?" I nod at the notebook.

"Of course, I will."

I pull Carol into my arms, just the way George C would do if he were here. "Thank you."

*

It's five o'clock. I'm downstairs, sitting at my mother's kitchen table in the Depot Street duplex for the first time ever. Mom isn't sitting yet. She's at the stove, stirring something in a big silver pot that smells savory and delicious.

"It's broccoli-cheddar soup. And I made bread," she says and then shrugs, as if she doesn't care what I think.

"First muffins, and now soup and bread? Are you trying to fatten me up?" It's the best I can do in the direction of civility. I'm a boat without a rudder, here in this kitchen. And the sea is rough. I have no direction.

She smirks. "Funny. But you *are* nothing but skin and bones."

Well, I'm a scarecrow—what do you expect? I smirk. But I don't explain this to her. She'd never get it.

But you get it, reader, don't you? You understand how it has come to this—a stiff and skinny scarecrow of a son, in a home that's not a home, staring at the standoffish mother who long ago rejected him. Tell me you understand how I ended up here.

Mom pours the soup into two plain white bowls and places them across from each other on the table's two rubbery, floral placemats, one of which was once meant for Jake but is now being used by me. Then she pulls a foil-wrapped loaf of bread from the oven with her fingertips. *This is the treatment Jake has been getting for years.* But again, I keep my mouth shut.

After cutting the warm bread on a plastic board beside a small plate of butter, she says, "Dig in." There's no enthusiasm in her voice. Zero warmth. Just two words echoing in the silent kitchen. A kitchen that, strange enough, smells like a place any hungry boy would want to be at dinnertime.

For a few seconds, I'm too pissed off to eat. But it smells so good. I finally break down and do as she said.

"You're probably wondering where Jake is." Again, Mom speaks as if she doesn't care much what I wonder about. She even yawns before taking a small bite of soup. I learned to be aloof from the very best teacher, didn't I?

I shrug in complimentary unresponsiveness, as I detest the sound of that man's name, not to mention the simple idea of him. Because, you see, thinking of him reminds me of my mother's unforgivable lack of compassion.

"I asked him to leave."

"You told me this morning." I can't look at her. Instead, I study the soup. I think she made it from scratch. The broccoli is unevenly chopped. The cheese is a little bit lumpy. I dissolve a salty hunk with my tongue.

"I want to explain."

"Go ahead." The bread she made is a work of art. And the taste—sweet and buttery, even without butter. The outer edges are crisp and the inside is soft...this bread is just like me. I find my anger growing. "I'm not gonna stop you."

My mother takes a deep breath and pushes her bowl off the placemat to the center of the table as if my very presence has managed to kill her appetite. "It's like this—I had you young. Even younger than *you* are now. The guy who knocked me up...*your daddy*...well, he bolted. Told him I was pregnant, I did, and he disappeared in the night."

I nod once. *Disappeared in the night.* I have some experience with that. George C escaped into the darkness too. My mother's gaze weighs on my face like a heavy, wet blanket pressed over my nose and mouth, making it hard for me to breathe.

She probably wants me to say something to comfort her. Like how it's okay she left me all alone to raise myself because she gave birth to me when she was just a girl. And that I don't mind at all how she let her perverted boyfriend lust over me and pressure me for sex for years on end, until, bit by bit, I morphed into the heartless thing I am now. But nothing comes to mind except, "It must have been fucking nice to have been Jake, eating homemade soup and bread for years when I was chowing down peanut butter sandwiches alone in my bedroom."

Looks like I'm kind of stuck on the whole "food is comfort" thing, huh? I'm also getting ahead of her touching little story, so I shut the fuck up and wait for more of her excuses.

She takes a breath and continues. "Anyhow, I went to work, and put you in the cheapest daycare in town. It was rough being so young with so much responsibility, Donovan. By the time Jake came around years later, I was tired. And he lifted some of the burden off me. We got a house together, and I got a car, and we ate and lived better, you know?"

"*I* didn't live better, Mom."

She sniffs. "I know that now."

"You knew that then."

And now she sighs. "I did...I just didn't want to be alone again."

Mom wouldn't have been alone; she had me. But I clearly wasn't enough. "So you let me be stared at and harassed by your loser boyfriend for years on end."

Mom stands and takes her bowl to the sink. I'm forced to stare at her back, which is probably for the best. I can't stand to gaze into her traitorous eyes.

I put the bitter frosting on the cake with one line. "And *I* was the one left alone."

"What do you want me to say? I screwed up, okay? I chose to do what would be easier on *me*!" She rinses the bowl. "But you were such a strong little boy— I figured you'd put Jake in his place. I told myself, 'Donovan will fix his wagon, and it'll all turn out okay.'"

I jump to my feet causing the chair to fly backward onto the floor behind me. "I was only ten years old when he started harassing me!"

She whips around to face me. "Even then, you were stronger than me."

My mouth falls open. I can't believe she put the responsibility of structuring our dysfunctional "family" dynamics into the hands of a child and a pervert.

"You were never an easy child, you know. You *made* people listen to you—even me. And so I figured...I figured you could take care of yourself with Jake." Her eyes are full of tears, but I feel no pity. "I can't change the past."

"No, you can't." This is the sad truth of the situation.

"But I can admit I was wrong. I can try to do better in the future. And the most important thing is, *you* can have a better life."

I shake my head. "My life was moving in a better direction..."

"But then George left?"

"That's about the size of it." I pick up the chair from the floor and sit.

She pulls in a breath, as if to speak, blows it out and then does it again. In an odd high-pitched tone I've never heard before, she squeaks, "Do you want to find him?"

I study her eyes for the first time since I arrived. And it's like looking in a fucking mirror. They're clear and blue, without a speck of innocence or sweetness to be found. The picture of distrust. And guilt. And a lot of pain.

"Let me help you," she says again, and I notice something else. There's a glimmer of hope buried deep in the lovely shade of blue. And it's a very good look on her.

"Okay, you can help," I reply, before I have a chance to change my mind. "Although I have no idea what good you can do. And it doesn't mean we're friends. It also doesn't mean I forgive you."

She nods. "That's fair."

"Come up to my place tomorrow night...for coffee." I invite her upstairs knowing I'll feel more confident in my own surroundings. "We can talk about where he could have gone then. But...but I have a feeling he's still around."

"I'll be there. I'll bring dessert." She comes to the table and reaches for my bowl.

"Wait, Mom. I want to finish my soup. And eat some more bread." I drag my chair back to the table. I haven't had a home-cooked dinner in too long to remember. I'm damn well going to eat it.

My mother sits across from me at the kitchen table and smiles. But her eyes seem sad.

Sunday

I GO INTO work half an hour before my shift starts because I need to deliver George C's message to Carlo. Thankfully, Monty is also there when I arrive. It's likely Carlo is going to need his help in the kitchen since George C won't be coming to work today. Or ever again.

In the break room, I don't have to deal with the bustle of changing shifts, as nobody is here yet. I pull my hair into a ponytail, switch my shoes, tie my apron around my waist, but don't bother to do the lipstick thing. Don't ask me why—I just don't. Instead, I hurry onto the restaurant floor to find Carlo.

They're sitting together in a booth, sipping hot drinks, which is kind of perfect. I can tell both of George C's bosses at once and they can figure out how to handle his absence together.

"Hey, you guys got a minute?" I'm not usually one for conversation, so they both seem surprised I initiated it.

"Of course, Donovan. Please sit down," Carlo says, moving toward the window. I slide into the booth beside him.

"You're early this morning." Monty signals Rhonda to refill his coffee. "What's on your mind?"

I'm out of my league right now. With my bosses, I try to be invisible, and if I can't be that, I go with being withdrawn, but polite. And here I am requesting their time and attention. "It's about George C."

"You two usually show up for work together. At least you have been lately. But I don't see him. Is he sick?" Carlo glances around.

"He isn't coming to work today. He *can't* come, actually."

Monty's thick eyebrows knit together. "And why did George C not call in sick himself?"

"He's not sick, sir."

"Then it looks like he's fired." Monty shakes his head. "It's a shame. I thought he was going to work out for us."

Carlo isn't as ready to fire George C without an explanation. "Just a minute, Monty. Let's hear the rest of what Donovan has to say."

Rhonda approaches the table and refills Monty's mug. "More coffee, Carlo?" she asks.

He shakes his head, and she moves to the next table with the coffee pot in hand.

"Thanks, sir," I say to Carlo. "There's more to the story. George C is in trouble with some bad guys in the area. They threatened him. And me...and so he felt he had to leave town to keep us safe." I don't want to spill all of George C's personal secrets, so I try to keep it vague.

"What kind of trouble?" Monty asks, foiling my plan.

"Uh, the kind of trouble that started when this guy, Billy, made him do shit he didn't want to do...with men...for money. And when he said he wasn't gonna do it anymore...uh, Billy wasn't exactly pleased."

Carlo lifts his hands to his cover his mouth. "Oh, dear. Poor George C."

Monty reaches across the booth to squeeze Carlo's shoulder. "Why don't you go check to see if Braxton can handle the kitchen on his own for a while, Carlo? I'll be in to help after I finish talking to Donovan."

"Yes. Good idea." I stand to let Carlo slide out of the booth, and then I sit across from Monty again. "In fact, m-maybe *I'll* throw on my apron and g-give him a hand today." I've never seen Carlo so shaken.

"Very good, sweetheart. You do that." Monty watches as Carlo walks toward the kitchen. "My Carlo is sensitive when it comes to this type of issue."

I nod but don't ask why.

"Now that he's gone, though, we can talk details." He runs his hand through the tuft of black hair that has fallen onto his forehead. "You said the guy's name is Billy. You know, George C's pimp."

I blow out a mouthful of breath. *Pimp* is hard to hear, but it's the right word. "Yeah. And this Billy-guy sent a couple of thugs after George C, to let him know he had to go back to work for him. When George C refused, they beat him up, but it didn't change his mind. When they figured out where I live—since he's been staying at my place—they threatened to hurt *me* if George C didn't go back to working for Billy, or leave town."

"How do you know all of this?"

"George C wrote me a letter."

Monty is quiet for a minute. He runs his hand though the tuft of hair, over and over, as he thinks. "It just so happens that I know a guy named Billy who hangs out at one the nightclubs downtown."

"Do you think it's the same Billy?"

"I wouldn't be surprised." Monty stands. "I'll have a word with him."

"But George C is already gone."

"I guess it's up to you to find him, then. When or if you do, call or text me. In the meantime, I'll see what I can do to straighten this thing out." Monty pulls a business card out of his wallet and hands it to me. "Use this phone number."

"Thanks, Monty." I address him by name, probably for the first time.

"You're a good friend to George C."

I shrug. I don't know if I'm much of a friend to George C. I hated him at this time yesterday, but here I am doing what I think is in his best interest. "I better get to work."

*

After my shift, I return to the break room to change and dump my tips into my messenger bag. A few of the other servers stand at their lockers near me as they get ready for the evening shift.

"Hey, Liss." Walter walks up to me. He comes closer to my side than ever before. Apparently, I've lost the intimidation factor since I publicly bonded with George C.

"What do you want?" I don't look at him. I may have melted, but I remember how the game is played.

"I heard rumors. Well, Rhonda overheard some of what you said to Monty, and she told me why George C is gone."

I sigh. "Nothing is private around here."

"I just wanted to say I'm going to miss the guy. He was pretty cool."

I turn my head just enough to glace at him, to study his slicked back hair that's supposed to make him appear classy, and notice the genuine regret in his eyes. "He *was* pretty cool."

"And, you know, he told me you're a decent guy, underneath it all. George C said you've had it hard in your life, and I should give you a break."

"A break?"

"Yeah. A break from my big mouth and my bad attitude."

"Oh, I see." George C was looking out for me here, too. "Well, don't do me any favors."

"I'm not doing it for you, so much. It's kind of a favor to George C." Walter pulls his jacket off. "I hope he comes back someday."

I wait for Walter to walk away before I say, "Me too."

*

I wonder if Mom is as nervous as I am when she knocks on the door to the second floor.

"Come in," I say and, without a hello, place two full mugs on the coffee table.

She puts a plate of brownies between them. "Thanks for letting me come over."

"Well, I want to find George C." Maybe she'll have an idea for how to go about it because Christ knows I have none.

Mom picks up her mug and takes a sip. "Do you know why he left?" No small talk. She cuts right to the chase, and I'm kind of glad. "Warm and fuzzy" is not a phrase that accurately describes our relationship.

"I have a good idea. Some guys were after him because they felt he owed them...something. He had to leave town or pay them back. He just couldn't do what they were asking of him."

"Is he dealing drugs, or doing them?"

"No. It isn't that."

She leans forward and pushes the plate toward my mug. "Have a brownie, Donovan. They're still warm." This comment comes out of nowhere. We suck at communicating, as you can see.

I glance at Mom. She's hiding the lower half of her face behind the mug, underlining the hardened expression in her eyes. "Not right now," I reply. This isn't a brownie and hot beverage party. It's a search party.

She gets right back to business. "When and where did you last see him?"

"It was here, after work on Friday night. He was gone in the morning."

"And why do you think he's still in the area?"

"Because on Saturday he left me a note at a thrift store we shopped at together. And the lady there thinks he's still around. She told me she senses it."

"Maybe you should leave *him* a note there."

"I did. I told him to come home." This conversation is getting us nowhere fast.

"Which thrift store?" Mom's not giving up.

"It's called Second Chance Thrift Shop."

"I know where it is. I'm off work tomorrow, so maybe I'll stop by and check if he's lingering in the neighborhood." She yawns, sending a message that it's no big deal how she's going to spend her day off searching for *my* long-lost friend.

"Can you also ask the cashier, a lady named Carol, if he left me another note? I can't get over there tomorrow. I have school and then work."

"I don't see why not." She slurps her coffee. I fight the urge to roll my eyes. Being critical comes naturally to me. "Has he met anyone from your school?"

"*You* know I don't do friends," I spit out, but then I stop and think. "He *has* met the members of the literary magazine staff."

"Why don't you put word out with them that George is missing? And if they come across him, they should let you know."

"That's as good an idea as any." I pick up my coffee and suck down half, ignoring the heat as it burns a path down my throat.

"Now have a brownie, son. They were your favorite when you were little." She knows me well enough to glance away as I reach for a brownie. It's a pride thing and she gets it.

*

I can smell him on my bedsheets. It's weird because I never noticed he had a specific scent before, but now that he's gone, it's everywhere. I can't get away from it, not that I want to. I flip onto my belly and press my face into the pillow, inhaling deeply the sweetness that was George C.

A single pillow on the bed. The funny thing is, although there were two of us, it never hit me that we needed another pillow because we shared so well. I used the pillow, and he used my belly. Or he used the pillow, and I used his shoulder. We really only needed one pillow in our double bed.

Once again, I turn over so I'm flat on my back staring at the ceiling. I don't refer to it as *my* bed because it never really was. And it hurts to think of it as *our* bed because now it isn't. I can't win, can I? All I can do is turn over and back, sighing deeply, unable to cry.

Maybe it's because I still have hope I'll see him again. Or maybe, without George C, I'm a freezer pop.

"My other half is certainly my better half." I say it aloud in the empty bedroom. It seems like the kind of thing a grandpa would say about a grandma in his trembling old man's voice, after fifty years of wedded bliss. But George C really *was* turning into my better half. Ask anyone who knew us both—my mother, Monty and Carlo, the kids at work, the Portals staff—they'd all say he was cuter and sweeter and kinder than me. Probably smarter. Friendlier. Softer. Warmer. Better. He really was my better half.

You think so too, and don't try to deny it.

I rise from the bed as, clearly, I'm unable to fall asleep here. There are no longer any monsters in this bedroom, but maybe I'll try the couch, like I did last night. I managed to catch a few hours of sleep there.

Once I'm settled on the couch, I pull the hairy yellow pillow against my chest and wrap my ankles around the purple one and close my eyes.

You know, reader, what bothers me most about George C being gone isn't how badly I miss him, although I do. Desperately. What pains me is my worry over him. Where is he? Is he safe? Is he warm? Is he lonely? Hungry? Tired? Sick?

Where is my better half, George C?

He isn't a scarecrow like me. He's soft and human and can't survive alone in a field in the pelting rain.

Monday

"ARE YOU FOR real, Van? An emergency meeting of the Portals Literary Magazine staff?"

"Called by the newest member—the staff illustrator?"

"At Moon Beams Coffee House?"

"What is this—some kind of joke?"

As soon as school let out, I texted all eight of the literary magazine staff.

EMERGENCY PORTALS LIT MAG MEETING!!!

4:00–4:45 PM Monday @ Moonbeams Coffee House

I'm calling you together to discuss an urgent matter. Break your back to get there.

The good news is all eight of them show up. The bad news: they don't seem overly thrilled. But they're here. And I have taken the advice of my mother for the first time, maybe ever.

"Thanks for showing up," I say and do my best to meet their collective questioning gaze with a haughty glare. Body language, I'll add, is a fascinating thing: Hands on hips, sarcastic smirks, hips jutted out to the side. All indicative of impatience, frustration, and annoyance. "I have something really important to talk to you about."

Tad easily slips back into *speak first, think later* mode. "What—did you drop your crayons into the toilet, and you need us to help you plunge them out? Because I had to cut out of soccer practice early for this. And we're in championships!"

Veronica sends him a stern glance. "What Tad means is our time is valuable. Not one of us isn't overscheduled to the max. We have jobs, sports, clubs, and tons of homework. So..."

Maria finishes. "So this had better be good."

I blurt it out. Nervously. Which is, you may be thinking, very unlike me, but whatever. "George C has gone missing."

Alex glances up from his Spanish workbook. "George C—is he that kid who drew the boots for my short story?"

Maria answers for me. "Yes. That's George C."

"He's supposed to draw two more pairs of shoes for me," Alex whines. "He *can't* be missing."

Mandy is the first one to show she possesses any heart at all. "What do you mean when you say George C is missing? Is something wrong?"

"What I mean is he disappeared. And I'm worried about him."

The members of the group exchange glances.

"Do you think he's hurt?" Mandy asks.

"Or been abducted?" Tad pipes in. "Not by aliens, but by a criminal. Like on TV."

"I don't know. But I'm looking for him. And I wanted to put the word out with you guys—if you see him anywhere around town, call or text me. Right away." The tone of my voice isn't cold. It's not haughty or sarcastic. It's what you'd probably call "desperate and needy." I'm not sure whether I care if the Portals Literary Magazine staff realizes this.

"Well, I can speak for the entire group when I say we will all keep our eyes open for him," Veronica says, as usual, stepping forward as the leader.

Alex still seems anxious, and I know he's guiltily worrying about the other two drawings for his short story. I want to be pissed off, but I kind of get it. This magazine is important to him. Shit, it's important to me too, but not in comparison to how important George C is.

"Thanks for showing up," I tell them again.

The body language has changed. Heads are hanging.

"We just hope he turns up. I know you guys are best friends; it must be really hard," Maria says. "Good luck in your search, Van."

One by one, the staff members hug me and then file out of the café.

Did you hear what I said? I received *eight* heartfelt hugs from *eight* self-important teenagers. And I stuck around for each and every last one of them.

My conclusion is that I'll go to any length to find George C.

*

I'm frustrated because Monty wasn't at the diner, so I got no news as to whether he'd spoken to the guy named Billy at the nightclub. And it's frigging cold outside; I have no clue if George C is going to sleep inside a warm house, in somebody's parked car, or outside on a park bench.

I'd hoped George C had moved in with Nikki again and was planning to question her about it at work. But when I arrived, she was in the break room, crying her eyes out over the fact that he's missing, so my hope George C was safe with Nikki was more of a pipedream.

My mother might be my only possible source of information about George C today. It's a total long shot, but since it's all I've got, I knock on her door instead of going straight upstairs when I get to our place.

The door is unlocked. "Mom?" I call as I push it open.

"Donovan, come in." She pulls a white dish from the microwave. "Have you eaten dinner? I just so happen to be heating up some chicken and rice from earlier."

"You made me dinner again, didn't you?" It sounds like an accusation, but since I haven't eaten anything since lunch, I sit at the kitchen table and try like hell not to drool.

Mom answers by placing a plate of food and a fork in front of me.

"Did you find out anything at Second Chance Thrift Shop today?" I ask between bites of chicken.

"As a matter of fact, I did." She slides the notebook out of her purse and opens it in front of me. "Does this have significance to you?"

And there in front of me is a decorative drawing of a pair of ballet slippers clearly created by nobody but George C. Tiny hearts and flowers and smiley faces cover every inch of the shoes, which makes me smile. "Yes. George C drew that." I turn the page to find a pair of men's leather loafers in the same style. "And this." The relief at receiving this communication from George C is intense. He hasn't frozen to death or starved or been murdered by the mob. I actually drop my fork, and it clangs on the side of the plate. I turn the page again, hoping for a note from him. But there's nothing.

"I hope you don't mind... I looked at your notes to each other."

"No, it's okay." I pick up the fork. "You're trying to help me."

"Well, I noticed he wrote back to you where you asked him to come home."

I turn back several pages, and there it is.

I can't come home. I want to, but they'll hurt you if I do, Vanny. And I'm hiding, so it's okay. They won't find me. Please don't worry.

I'm trying to find the courage to leave town for good so both of us can be safe. I just can't make myself go yet. You're here, and even if I'm not in the same room as you, I'm near you as long as I'm in town. I miss you badly.

George C

I don't want my eyes to tear up, but they do.

"If you want to write to him, I can drop the notebook at Second Chance on my way to work tomorrow morning. You know; if you want me to."

"That would be great. Thanks. I'll write something and bring it down to you early tomorrow morning before school."

"Very good. Now finish your dinner. Would you like a glass of milk?"

"Um, sure. And do you have any more of those brownies from last night?"

"I have a few," she replies.

"Cool. I won't keep you long."

"You can stay as long as you like." She tilts her head and studies me as if she's seeing me for the first time. And I realize my head is tilted too, and that I've never seen the woman standing before me.

Tuesday

I STUFF ONE hundred dollars in twenties from my emergency fund into an envelope and tape it to the next page in the notebook. And I write a note beneath it.

The better half of me wants you to leave town so you'll be safe. The selfish half of me is glad you're still nearby.

Please buy a warm coat and a scarf and some gloves with this money. Or a night in a cheap hotel room. It'll make me worry less if I know that wherever you are, you're warm.

George C—I'm not one to make dramatic declarations about my innermost feelings, but if I was, I'd say I miss you so much I find it hard to sleep.

And thanks for the pictures of shoes. Alex is going to cry with relief.

Van

I slide the notebook under Mom's front door. I'm not in the mood for an emotional morning discussion.

*

Thanks to the size of his hair, I find Alex easily in the hallway before school and give him the shoe illustrations. He actually does shed a few tears of joy.

*

"Donovan, can you come to the breakroom when you have a minute?" Monty shows up near the end of my shift with a question that makes me shudder with anticipation.

"Yeah, sure. Let me bring a few checks to customers, and I'll be right in."

No waiter has ever hurried his customers to pay for their dinners as rudely as I do tonight. I don't care if I cause them serious indigestion, and I get no tips. Monty has news, and I need it right fucking now.

I rush to the back room and find him sitting on the purple couch. I want so much to play it cool, but it doesn't happen. "Did you find Billy? What did he say?"

"Listen, kid. I've made contact with Billy, but we haven't sat down together to talk yet. There's progress, though, so keep your chin up. Have you figured out where George C is?"

"Not yet. I'm working on it. I have an idea for something I can do, but I'll probably be a little late to work tomorrow. Is that okay?"

"Yes, of course. Take an extra hour. I'll get one of the afternoon servers to stay late."

"Thanks."

Monty stands and hugs me hard enough to break me in half. I must resemble a teddy bear lately, considering the number of heartfelt embraces I've been receiving. Ugh—don't try to suggest, my fine reader, that I enjoyed them. "We're going to work this thing out, Donovan. I can feel it in my bones."

My bones are creaking because Monty apparently doesn't know his own strength. "Sure, we are." I do my best to sound enthusiastic, but I'm not sure I pull it off.

Wednesday

AFTER SCHOOL, I head straight to the Second Chance Thrift Shop. My plans involve lingering and loitering, and if that gets me nowhere, I'll take the direct approach.

It's early November and, frankly, it's frigid outside. I'm glad for my bus pass so I don't have to walk all the way there in the cold, although on warmer days, I don't mind a long walk or run. For all I know, George C spends his nights in the bus station trying to keep his ass from freezing.

I grab a cup of coffee to go at the first café I come to, hoping it will warm my insides while I conduct covert operations outside of the thrift store. Then the loitering begins. I walk deliberately up and down the sidewalk across the street, watching for the appearance of a brown-haired boy with sensitive eyes. After an hour, the only part of my body not frozen solid is the hand clutching the now lukewarm cup.

I cross the street to view the store and its surroundings from a different angle. Again, I pace. I don't linger when I pass the store, though, afraid Carol will notice me before I'm ready. After another forty-five minutes of this avoidance game, I'm ready for the direct approach. If I don't take the direct approach, it's possible I'll freeze to death.

Chilled to the bone, I enter the thrift shop and get figurative cold feet to add to my literal ones when I see Carol. I'm not sure if she sees me before I scramble to the back of the store to gather my courage. After killing time in the book section, I come closer to the front of the shop and lurk behind the men's coat rack, waiting for Carol to be alone.

When no customers are in sight, I approach the cash register. "I know you've seen him," I say. "So tell me where he is."

Carol clears her throat. She peers at my feet instead of my face, which is weird because she's a direct sort of person. "I don't know what you mean."

"Did he leave anything for me today?"

"Not today, son." It seems like she wants to say more, but covers her mouth with her hand to stop it from coming out. "Why don't you check back here after school tomorrow?"

"You know where George C is. It's obvious."

Carol turns away from me. "Is there anything else I can help you with today?"

"Nope. You helped me enough."

Carol shakes her head. "Maybe he's afraid to be with you. Maybe he's worried about your safety."

"Maybe I'm worried about *his* safety," I counter.

"Well, if there isn't anything else, I need to steam some girls' holiday dresses now." Carol steps out from behind the cash register and walks to the children's department.

I know what I have to do. But I rush off to work so I'm not more than an hour late.

Thursday

SCHOOL SEEMS TO last forever. Work takes even longer. But Carlo was cool and let me come in right after school today, so I can leave at five thirty. I'm out the diner's front door before 5:31 p.m., and no more than two minutes later, I flag down a cab to one block away from the Second Chance Thrift Shop. I get out and do what I've been doing a lot of lately: I lurk in the shadows, watching the comings and goings at the thrift store. The success of my plan is a total long shot. But it's also my *only* shot. I'm going to give it everything I've got. I hope it's enough.

Naturally, Carol is the last worker to leave the shop on the coldest day so far this year—the day during which

I play at being a spy. When she locks the door, it's the moment of truth. If she heads around to the parking lot in back of the store, I'm shit out of luck because if she gets in a car and drives away, there's not a chance in hell I can follow. I doubt she'll grab a cab; it would be too expensive a form of transportation for her to use on a daily basis. And if she goes to the bus stop, I'll pull my hoodie up over my rather distinctive hair and slip onto the bus just before it starts to move and hope like hell she doesn't see me.

It must be my lucky day. The best-case scenario unfolds before me. Carol turns left outside the store entryway, pulls her puffy red down coat tightly around her, and starts to walk. From a safe distance, I follow along.

Carol seems to suspect she isn't alone. Several times, she slows down and turns around to check if someone is following her. Each time, I'm able to dart into a doorway, behind a mailbox, or down an alley to hide.

Carol isn't street-smart at all, not that I am. And I sincerely hope I'm the only one who came up with the bright idea to follow her in search of a certain boy.

We walk along the main street sidewalk for fifteen minutes, and then we turn down a side road called Anderson Ave. Carol heads up the stairs in front of a dilapidated, single-family home jammed between two large apartment buildings. She glances around one more time. As she starts to unlock the door, someone inside pulls it open. That someone is George C.

It takes every ounce of my self-control not to jump out from behind the metal trash can on the corner where I'm hiding, point at him, and scream, "Aha! I found you!" and then race up the stairs, push Carol aside, and pull my long-lost friend into my arms with the intention of never letting him go. But I don't. I play it cool—and yes, I'm just playing because I'm actually sweating my ass off with anticipation on this fine subzero evening. I will admit to drinking in the sight of him as he stands, smiling, in Carol's doorway.

When Carol is safely inside and the door has clicked shut, I drop to my knees on the city street. It's relief that brings me down. I'm not angry at George C for leaving me anymore. And before you ask, I'm not exactly pleased with him, but I know he did what he thought he had to do. I recognize that he was misguided by fear, but his heart was in the right place. And who the hell am I to criticize somebody's overreaction to fear? My life story has been written in response to my own personal terror.

Now it's time to swallow my pride; I must knock on the door and beg George C to open it and let me inside so I can return to the land of the living again. Maybe I'm being dramatic, reader, but I got to live in human company for a few weeks, and I liked it. When George C moved in, the monsters moved out. He made me believe I was strong enough to cope, and so, just like that, I did.

Don't call me a drama queen, you hear? It may be dramatic, but it's how I see it, which is really all that matters.

I allow Carol fifteen minutes to take her coat off and get settled, maybe even to start dinner, before I climb the stairs to her tiny home. I stand on the front door landing, panting and sweating and slightly nauseated, for at least five full minutes before I find my balls and knock. Then I step to the side so they can't see me through the peephole.

"Who is it?" It's Carol's voice. She sounds scared and protective.

"Get George C!" I shout.

"Not until you show your face...and tell me who you are."

I'm certain that, already, gallant George C has gently pushed Carol aside, and his eye is at the peephole. I know this because I know him. He's brave, even at his own peril. I step directly in front of the door.

"Van!" It's George C's voice. I'd know it anywhere.

"Please let me in... I need to talk to you. Please!"

"Did anybody follow you here?" he asks.

"No. I was the one doing the following tonight."

And the door slowly opens to George C and Carol, huddled together, anxious and confused. "You followed me home, young man?" she asks, and our gazes lock. The expression in her eyes isn't warm.

"I had to see him."

"I told you to check back at the store tomorrow," she argues.

"I know George C, and I thought maybe he'd sneak out of your house tonight in the middle of the night the way he left mine." I glance from Carol to him. "And I couldn't risk losing you again."

His eyes are more striking than I remember. The color of ash—and solemnly sincere. But still, they give nothing away. I can't see the shame he wrote of in his letter. I can't see fear of rejection *or* discovery. I can't see the love for me he hinted at.

I'm going to have to earn his confidence—this is the only thing that is clear to see.

When he reaches out, I'm not sure if he's going to push me away or pull me in. But George C grabs me by the neck of the plaid flannel shirt I wear over my hoodie and drags me into the house, and then into his arms. I've never felt so happy to be anywhere in my life.

"George C." It comes out on a breath. Carol may think it's a sound of anguish, but it's a breath of relief. Of painful reentry to the world. "You left me, George C."

"I...had to." He can barely speak; maybe his throat is as tight as mine. "Van, I still *have* to."

"You don't have to go. We can fix this together."

"Billy won't give up. He'll find me, and then he'll find you, and he'll hurt us both."

"I took a chance. I trusted you." I'm going to beg now. But I hold my head high and do it right. "Please. Take a chance on me. *Please.*"

Carol clears his throat. "George, why don't you take Van to your room. You can talk in private there. I'll be in the kitchen making dinner." I'm not convinced this is what she actually wants, but it's what she says.

George C releases me, but I can't let go. I'm scared shitless I'll lose him. I cling to his neck until he pushes me back. "Let's talk in my room."

Still, I hang on to his arm. My fingers dig into his flesh. You see, reader, my participation in the land of the living requires this man's presence, so I refuse to let go. Thank Christ he doesn't make me. Instead, he leads me down a narrow hallway into a shoebox of a bedroom. The shades are pulled down and it's dark, but I can't miss his backpack and a kitchen trash bag stuffed full of his clothes in the corner of the room. The bed is neatly made. We sit together on it.

"You know about me...and about what I did." His voice is raspy with emotion.

"Yes, I know about what you *had* to do...I read your letter."

"What I did...was one of the reasons I was able to make myself leave. I knew I'd never have to tell you about it if I was gone." This is nothing short of a confession, and I appreciate the candor.

"I'm glad I know." Truthfully, I'm incredibly relieved to know why he was so secretive, and it wasn't that he didn't trust me. He felt he had done something unforgivable. "We've all done shit we had to do, or thought we had to do. Shit we regret."

He sniffs. I don't want to see him to cry, although I won't try to stop him. After all, he let me lose control when I needed to. "But you've never done something like *that*...I let two guys, you know, *do* me. For money—I sold myself.

"You did what you felt you had to and you survived it. It's all I care about. You survived, and you were able to help me survive."

He falls into me. I finally find the courage to let go of his wrist to wrap my arms around his shoulders. I'm being strong for him, and it fills me with an emotion I've never before experienced. I'm worth something—there's a reason I'm alive.

Again, it's dramatic, but I'm not sorry.

"Someday, we'll make love, and it'll wipe away all the memories that hurt you. The thoughts that make you feel worthless will be gone." He has done this for me, and I'm sure I can return the favor. And it will be amazing.

He pushes me back. His eyes glisten in the light from the hallway. "We've already made love. Every time we got close to each other in our bed, I knew what making love was *supposed* to be."

"Think of it like this. You and me—we're more than the worst thing we've ever done."

In the darkness, his gaze on my face is thick and heavy and solid. It's not going anywhere. "What do you mean?"

"I've acted cold and callous, and I've even tried to scare people—for years on end—but it isn't who I really am. And you tried to pay back what you *thought* was a debt to a very bad man, but the action you took to pay it isn't who you are."

"You're right. I believe you," George C says.

"Good."

"We're stronger together, aren't we?" he asks.

"*I* think so."

"But I still need to leave."

His words hit me like a bullet to my chest. I can hardly catch my breath. "What?" I fall back on the bed. "*What?*"

"Our feelings for each other are everything I ever hoped for, but they don't change the facts. Billy will hurt us if I stick around." He stretches out beside me. "I can't let anything happen to you."

"Nothing will happen. Monty thinks he knows who Billy is. And he thinks he can talk some sense into him."

"He and Carlo know what I did?"

"You gave me permission to tell them. You said so in the letter."

George C nods. "Were they disgusted?"

"No. They were concerned. Before you leave, can't you wait and see if Monty can help?"

"I guess it can't hurt. Carol likes having me here, and she said I can stay until I figure things out."

"Then it's settled."

George C wraps himself around me, and I shiver in the good way. "Nothing is settled. All I'm agreeing to is I won't leave until we find out if Monty can somehow help. But I don't have a clue how he can."

"Fine. And if he can't help us, then I'll leave with you."

George C sits up. "You can't leave home. You won't graduate from high school."

I sit beside him so he can read the honesty in my eyes. "I'm eighteen years old. I can do what I choose to do. And I need your promise you'll never take off on me again. I need a promise."

He gets off the bed and walks to the window, pulls open the shade, and stares outside into the darkness. But he doesn't promise me a thing.

I follow him to the window and rest my hands on his shoulders. And then I make my confession. "I don't do too great of a job in the realm of human interaction without you around." I grit my teeth like I used to all the time, but haven't felt the need as much since I met George C. And it's hard to say this because I'm a confirmed loner. But I say it anyway. "I need you with me. Promise that whatever we do, we'll do it together."

He turns around and looks at me. In the dim lighting, I can't make out the expression in his eyes, but I *know* what it is. George C loves me. "I promise. We'll figure things out together."

When our lips meet, I come back to life, and it's better than before. The scarecrow's arms and legs and heart of wood turn to flesh, and I can suddenly feel everything I never let myself feel before.

*

Carol's beef stew is warm and thick and tastes like it was made with love. Sure, this sounds sappy, especially coming from a guy like me, but it's been an emotional day, so cut me some slack. Remember, bookworm, this sappy sentiment comes from a guy who hasn't eaten homemade beef stew in way too fucking long.

"How long have you been staying here with Carol?" I ask George C, who has pretty much dived into his bowl of stew too. He hasn't had much opportunity for home-cooked meals either.

"I've been here for the past three nights."

"And before that?"

"I slept in a vacant mill building." George C shudders at the memory, and I want to touch him. I want to tell him he'll never have to sleep out in the cold again.

"Shit. That must have purely sucked." I offer Carol a shrug of apology for my use of foul language. I'm not used to toning down my words for anybody. But Carol has done a lot for us, and I don't want to insult her. "Sorry, Carol, but it must have been super cold out there."

"Yes, I thought so too. And I insisted George stay with me when I learned he had nowhere else to go," Carol replies. "I have an extra bedroom and, well, I've enjoyed the company. It's been two years since my husband passed, and my daughter's family lives in Florida." She stops talking and pats her lips with her napkin. "It gets lonely sometimes."

Just sayin', reader, don't you think it's fucked up how so many people are lonely in life and don't really have to be? "Well, I'm glad George C and you hooked up."

"I am too, dear." Carol opens a plastic bag of rolls and takes out two. "Here. Soak up the stew with these, boys." She passes them to us, and we get back to eating.

After a few minutes, George C places his spoon beside his bowl. "So what's up with Monty and Billy? I mean, when do you think he's going to talk to him?"

"Soon, I hope."

George C shakes his head. "I don't know if it'll do any good. Billy made it clear. I do what he wants or leave town. I can't see his perspective changing."

"We just have to wait. If it doesn't work, we'll make a new plan." I can't stop myself from reaching under the table and squeezing George C's knee. I need to remind him as often as possible that we're in this together.

"I want to go to the Portals meeting with you tomorrow."

"Isn't it at Van's school?" Carol interjects. "I don't think it is safe for you to go there, George, until your boss speaks with that awful man."

"Carol, Billy's men think I'm long gone. There's no way they'll come looking for me at Windsor Academy."

I want him to come to the meeting with me so much I don't argue. "Take a taxi there. I'll meet you in the foyer of the school, and then I'll bring you back here before I have to go to work."

Carol seems worried. You'd think George C was her adopted son. "I don't know, boys…"

"I'll be fine. I really want to go. I want to see if they need any more drawings for the magazine."

He smiles in such a hopeful way that Carol nods. "I'll expect you to be back here when I get home from work."

And so it's decided. George C will meet me at school tomorrow just before three.

I don't want to leave Carol and George C after dinner, but my mother actually calls and asks me where I am. And when I'll be home. She seems to want to keep track of me these days.

Fucked up to the max, huh? You think I should stay? Hang on to the guy I came so close to losing? Well, shit, it crosses my mind, but I decide to indulge Mom's new and improved motherly instincts. You know, to dole out some positive reinforcement.

I kiss George C good-bye. "Can't wait 'til tomorrow."

Part Four: George C

Friday

I'M SCARED TO leave Carol's house, but I do because I told Van I'd meet him at Windsor Academy. It's not only that: I *want* to go to the Portal's meeting so much. I'm important there.

Until last night when he showed up on my doorstep, I didn't think I'd ever see Van again. I wanted to, but I never imagined a way it could work out. Over the three days I spent at Carol's house, I'd worked to prepare myself to leave town and to leave the person who so quickly came to mean everything to me. I was going to do it too. My tentative plan was to spend this morning cleaning Carol's refrigerator—it seriously needs it—and then washing and changing my sheets so it was like I'd never slept in her daughter's bed. Then I'd write her a thank-you/good-bye note, leave it on the kitchen counter, and slip out before she got home from work.

But here I am, on the bus to Windsor Academy to meet with the guy I think I can call my boyfriend. And like I said, I have another reason to risk life and limb by leaving the safety of Carol's house. I really want to go to the Portals Literary Magazine meeting. I want to hear from Alex, himself, about how he liked my drawings of shoes. And I want to volunteer to create more images. For the first time in forever, I'm confident about something other than being able to score some weed or bring the beer. I crave more of this new confidence.

I'm a few minutes early for our meeting, so I sit on the stone wall that separates a grassy area from the parking lot and watch the kids stream out of Windsor Academy, backpacks slung over their shoulders and chatting with one another about stuff most teenagers are concerned with. Like the high school football team's chance of winning the playoff game on Saturday, the lyrics to a Chance the Rapper tune, and the best place to grab a soy latte. Stuff I haven't had the luxury of worrying about for a few years because I was so busy staying wasted and hiding my sexuality, and, more recently, keeping warm at night.

At a few minutes before three, I walk to the entrance of the school and try to look casual as I stand and wait. Five, then ten minutes pass, and there's no sign of Van. And just like that, I'm certain something's wrong. Don't ask me how I know; I won't be able to give you a logical answer. All I can say is I know Van, and pure relief was in his eyes last night when he looked at me. He wouldn't be late to meet me today for anything.

Luckily, the preppy kid, Tad, from the literary magazine staff is also running late to the meeting. He must have run out for coffee between school and the meeting, because he's trying to run and not spill the contents of a paper cup, which isn't going well.

"Hey, Tad, right?"

He stops by the door. "Yeah. You're Van's friend...George C?"

"Uh-huh. He was supposed to sign me in for the meeting but, uh..." I'm certain he didn't forget about me. Something is wrong.

"No worries. I'll sign you in." He lets me into the school building and signs me in at the front desk.

Tad stops at his locker and then in the boys' restroom before we go to the meeting. I want to rush him along, but he got me into the school, so it's only polite to wait for him. When we get to room 221, I rush inside, still hanging onto a sliver of hope that Van will be sitting at one of the desks. But he isn't.

"Hey, George C. So glad you've been found," Veronica says. Then she glances at the clock above the door. "You're late, Tad."

"Better late than never," he replies.

"Your shoe pictures rocked," Alex offers and I smile.

"Where's Van? He's supposed to have about five rough images for us and a final draft of the front and back covers." Maria stands and walks to the doorway. She leans out of the room to glance around the corner.

"Maria, didn't I tell you? Van wasn't in school today," Veronica calls.

"This so sucks—we really need him."

Before Maria has a chance to sit, I say, "He promised he'd meet me in the front of the school right before three, and he never showed up."

"Well, he couldn't meet you if he was absent from school, could he?" Veronica has "duh" written all over her face.

"Did he call your cell phone?" Mandy asks.

"Um, I kind of lost track of it." I stand. "I've gotta go look for him."

"He's probably at his house," a girl whose name I don't know suggests.

"In his bathroom barfing," Tad adds.

"No...I'm sure something's wrong," I insist.

Veronica takes matters into her hands. "Look, *I'll* call him and put your mind to rest." She pulls her phone from her pocket and makes the call. "Hmmm. I think his phone is off. It went straight to voice mail."

"I've gotta go." I suspect Billy's teaching me a lesson by snatching Van. And I can't let anything happen to him. I scribble Carol's cell phone number on the back side of a homework paper I find on a desk. "If you see him, tell him to call this number." I leave it on the desk and run out of the classroom.

*

Once I'm on the street, I want to run wildly, screaming Van's name, but I have no real direction. It would be useless. After a few seconds of consideration, I decide to go to the Monty-Carlo Diner.

I use my last few bucks on a cab, and the ten-minute drive seems like an eternity. I jump out of the cab almost before it stops and then barge into the diner. "Monty!" The man is hard to miss, as he's almost six five. "Monty— I think Van is missing!"

"George C, where have you been? Donovan has been searching for you."

"I'm sorry I took off, but I'm back now, and we've got a serious problem. I think Billy had his guys pick up Van! He was supposed to meet me at his school, but he never showed up!"

"Did you call him?" Monty asks.

I didn't, but Veronica did. "It went straight to voice mail."

Carlo is listening from his seat in the booth closest to the front of the diner. "I have his emergency information on my phone. I'll call his mother and ask if he's at home."

I probably should have gone to Van's house to look for him first, but I was so certain he got snatched off the street I came straight here for help.

Carlo has a short chat with Van's mother, I assume, and then tells us, "Donovan left for school this morning as usual. His mother has no idea why he wasn't there."

"Oh, God." I drop my butt into the booth beside Carlo. "He *is* missing."

"Well, Nancy Liss is c-coming right over. We'll put our heads t-together and figure out where he is," Carlo says, his voice shaking.

The next ten minutes seems like ten years. Finally, Nancy shows up and she appears how I feel, worn-out and disheveled. "What's going on?" she asks.

Monty steps forward. "Let's all sit down and talk this out. I'm sure we can make sense of what happened to Van."

We join Carlo in the booth, and the discussion starts in earnest.

"Donovan left for school just like he always does this morning. I heard him come down the stairs at seven fifteen." Nancy's eyes are puffy and bloodshot, as if she's been crying. I can't help but wonder when she turned into mother of the year.

"He was supposed to meet me at his school just before three," I tell them.

Nancy shoots me a dirty look. "He spent the past week trying to find you, George. You finally decided to grace Donovan with your presence, and now he's gone. I highly doubt it's a coincidence."

"Well, he spent the past eight years trying to get *your* attention, Nancy," I retort because I'm angry. She seems to think she can blame me for his problems when she is the true source of most of them. But I *am* the reason he's missing, aren't I?

"Bickering isn't going to get us any closer to locating Donovan," Carlo reminds us, and he's right. "We need to focus."

Nancy and I offer each other curt nods, and then I shift my attention to Monty. "This guy, Billy, lives over in Williamsburg Heights." I glance at Nancy to include her. "He told me I had to leave town. But I stuck around... because I couldn't make myself move far away from Van. You know?"

Nancy's glare is sharp enough to slice paper. I can see she blames me, as I blame myself.

"He threatened to hurt me and Van if I stuck around."

"And you *stayed*?"

I stick my face in my hands and mumble, "I already know this is my fault. I know it..."

Monty redirects the conversation. "Listen, George C, describe this guy, Billy—in detail."

I clear my throat. "Well, Billy's about my size. He has a thin moustache and always wears a black leather jacket. He wears his hair a little bit shorter than mine, and he usually sticks it in a ponytail." It's easy for me to recall the details. He changed my life for the worse, and I can't forget him no matter how much I'd like to. "He's not a buff dude or anything. He's kind of skinny, actually."

"Black hair with a little gray on top and always wearing western boots?" Monty asks.

"Yeah."

"It's Billy Bartolow, like I suspected when Van mentioned him to me. I know the guy from way back. Slimy loser, that one is."

"Can you find the man—and talk some sense into him?" Nancy asks.

"I've been asking questions about him around town." Monty slides out of the booth. "Tonight, I'll stop by a bar where used to hang out. Billy was planted on a barstool there just about every night. I haven't stopped by for years, but if I know Billy, his habits haven't changed."

"I'm going with you," I say and slide out of the booth.

Monty shakes his head. "You're underage. There's no point in you tagging along."

Nancy points at Monty. "Then *I'm* going with you."

"You'll be the only woman in the place," he warns.

"Ask me if I care. Now, let's get going."

"It's too early—the place will be empty, and if we wait around for Billy all afternoon, we'll lose the element of surprise. Meet me back here at ten tonight."

"Fine." Nancy drags herself from the booth and storms to the door. "Just when I was getting to know my son again, *this* happens." She glares at me again, but then her anger seems to break. "If you want to come back to the house with me, George, it's fine with me."

Van's mom is moody, but even though she blames me, I think she still likes me. "Thanks, but I'm staying with a friend. I think she's expecting me home for dinner."

"Have it your way," she replies, and she's gone.

"You have a place to stay?" Carlo asks.

"Yeah, with a lady who I met at a thrift shop, if you can believe it."

"I'll drive you," Carlo offers.

"Thanks a lot." Tonight is going to be the longest night ever. I grab Monty by the sleeve of his button-down shirt. "Can you call me when you know anything about Van? I'm kind of worried sick." I grab a pen from the pocket of my hoodie, lean on the table, and scribble Carol's number on a napkin.

"I'll let you know as soon as I have any information."

*

Carol is probably the best person for me to be with when I'm as worried as I am tonight. She has a calming effect on me.

"You need to eat. Starving to death isn't going to help Van." She pushes an enormous bowl of rice and beans at me across the table.

"I really can't eat right now. I'm not feeling very well." All I can do is imagine Mayo and Jonah beating on Van the way they beat on me. Maybe Van talks tough, but he's not. He's got a soft heart, and he protects it with biting sarcasm. His bad attitude won't defend him from those guys' fists. His fear will grow and grow as they threaten him, and then they'll give him an excellent reason for his fear. Jonah and Mayo have no mercy; those two thugs take pride in making people beg. I don't know if Van will ever be the same if they hurt him.

And even though I doubt Billy would try to force Van into sex with a stranger, every minute we delay, there's more of a chance something like this will happen.

"Can I possibly borrow your cell phone tonight?"

"Why? You can't be considering going out and searching for Van. That would be dangerous."

I know where Billy lives, and Van is likely to be there. I need to find out for myself, not that I'm going to share my intention with Carol. "No," I lie, "I just want to go to the store and buy something for Van's apartment. You know, as a welcome home gift."

"You're going shopping? Then why do you need my cell phone?"

"Because Monty said he'd call me as soon as he talks to Billy, and I don't want to risk missing the call. *Please...*"

"You know I can't say no to you, dear. Take my phone and go shopping. It'll keep you from worrying too much."

"I hope so."

She slides her cell phone across the table. "Try to relax. I'm sure Van will be sleeping in his own bed tonight."

"I'm sure he will too," I say, even though I'm not. "And thanks." I snatch up the phone. Carol's eyes widen in alarm at my urgency, but I grin and wink, and she calms down.

"Take a few dollars from my purse. You'll need it."

*

I never thought I'd return to Billy's split-level ranch in Williamsburg Heights. At least not by my own free will. But here I am. Wonders never cease.

I linger by the stop sign on the street corner. It provides no cover for me, but like Nancy said at the restaurant, ask me if I care. Van's in trouble because of me, and I'll do anything to find him. I'll risk myself; I don't care.

It's weird how easily fear can be put into perspective. I was desperately afraid of Billy and his gang until I considered Van's fear when faced by their kind of evil. Now, I care nothing for myself.

In fact, I care so little that I march up the front stairs of Billy's house of horrors and knock on the door. The lights are on—inside and out. I fully expect someone to answer the door. Maybe Billy, himself. Or maybe one of his loser pals, Jonah or Mayo, will greet me with a punch in the nose. I hold my breath and wait, but nobody comes.

Breaking into the house crosses my mind, but Jonah once told me that Billy is the king of alarm systems. I wouldn't get very far, and I'd end up at the police station, which wouldn't help me find Van. So I trot down the stairs and along the sidewalk, walk past a few houses, where I finally drop to my butt on the sidewalk so I can concentrate on what to do next.

Carol's cell phone rings. I automatically pick it up. "Hello?"

"George C? It's Tad," says the voice on the other end.

"Tad?" Why would the preppy dude from the Portals meeting be calling me? "What's up?"

"Well, you said to ask him to call you if we saw Van. And I see Van, but he's in no shape to call."

"What do you mean?"

"Well, I found him on the street outside the bowling alley. An SUV was pulling away. I think they'd just dropped him off."

"Why is he in no shape to call me?"

"Something's off with him. Like, big time. I mean, he's not bloody or bruised or anything, but he's acting weird as fuck. He's in some kind of daze."

Billy got to him. "Where is he?"

"I'm with him at the Masco Valley Mall. I led him from the street into the mall, and I took him to the men's room. It was all I could think of to do."

"I'll be right over. Stay with him—you hear me?" I don't wait for him to answer. And since I have very little cash, I have to run there; I may need the money Carol gave me to catch a cab somewhere once I've got Van. But it's not too far; I can be there in less than ten minutes if I keep a steady pace. I have no idea what I'm going to do when I get there, though.

I know how you're feeling right now, reader, because I'm feeling the same way. You're emotionally exhausted from the constant turmoil. You're wondering, *when is this angst marathon going to come to an end?* All you want from this story is a torture cease-fire—maybe a quick glimpse of passion between the clean sheets on Van's bed, and a word or two of affection. Did it ever hit you I want that stuff too? But I've learned the hard way you can't always get what you want.

As I run, I picture Van, scared into a daze he may never come out of.

Can this actually happen? Can people get trapped in their fear and never find their way out? Don't answer... just know I never meant for anything bad to happen to Van.

I love him.

*

I'm completely out of breath when I get to the men's room at the bowling alley end of the Masco Valley Mall. "Where is he?" I shout at Tad, who is leaning against the far wall.

"In there," he answers and points toward the largest stall.

The door isn't locked, so I go right in. Van is kneeling on the floor, staring at the toilet. He's in the position of a person who is about to lose his lunch. "Hey, dude. You okay?"

Van doesn't seem to realize I'm here. He doesn't look up or nod, let alone answer me.

"Do you feel like you're gonna be sick?"

Nothing.

"Hey, Tad."

"Yeah?"

"Can you call us a cab? I'm gonna take him home."

"I can get you an Uber. Where are you going?"

I have to make a quick decision. Should I take him to Carol's house or to his home?

"We're going to 1539 Depot Street." Van needs to be in familiar surroundings. He may not actually *be* safer in his home, but he'll feel safer there. I just have to hope Monty's night is successful, and nobody comes looking for us.

A couple seconds later, Tad says, "I set it up and put it on my credit card."

"Thanks, man." I help Van to his feet. He's strangely cooperative. "I'll pay you back, I promise."

"Nah, don't worry about it."

I help Van out of the stall and get a good look at his face. His skin is as pale as I've ever seen it, and his eyes are different too. They seem dark and hollow—like if I gaze into them, I'll see right through to the bathroom's far wall. He stares straight ahead. He's in his own world.

"Just get Van back on his feet, okay?" Tad urges.

"I'm gonna try."

Tad and I each put an arm under one of Van's shoulders, and we help him to the street. When the Uber arrives, we sit him down, and Tad buckles his seat belt as I run around the car and get in the other side.

"Let me know what happens," Tad calls as we drive away.

I'll be honest with you; it's not my top priority.

*

Nancy is out when we get home, and I know it's for the best. She'd freak if she saw the way her newly valued son's eyes stare straight in front of him and shoulders sag as he floats up the walkway. I fish around in the front pockets of Van's jeans and find his apartment keys. We make our way inside, up the stairs, and into his apartment.

The couch or the bed? The bed or the couch? It has always been a major decision for us, but tonight, it's a decision of epic proportions. Is he seeing monsters that resemble Jonah and Mayo and Billy? Will being in the bedroom force his fears to the front of his mind? Maybe that's what he needs to get him to snap out of his daze—to face his fear. I really don't know because I have no clue what happened to him.

I put off the decision of where to sleep by leading Van to the bathroom, and then dampen a cloth and press it to his forehead. I have no idea why I do this; I guess I've seen it done to distressed and injured people in the movies. Next, I tug down his jeans without undoing the buttons and help him step out of each leg. His plaid flannel shirt and white T-shirt come off next. Once he's in just his boxers, he seems to know what to do. He pees and bends over the sink to rinse his hands and face. And then he waits for me to do the same things. Van lets me lead him to the bedroom.

I leave the light on, unsure as to whether the growing darkness will frighten him. Aren't monsters supposed to come out in the dark? Once I've tucked us both into his bed, we finally make eye contact. Van's head is on our single pillow, and he turns to glance my way with dark, empty eyes. When he swallows deeply, I realize even this minor connection with me is too much for him to bear.

"What did they do to you, Vanny?"

He shakes his head—just a little bit—and closes his eyes. I know what he's telling me. Now isn't the right time to talk.

So, instead of pushing the issue, I turn on my side to face him and move close enough to feel the warmth of his body. But I don't pull him against me. Van needs to be close enough to me to feel safe, but not too close, to feel smothered. I place my palm on top of his ice-cold hand and say, "Try to sleep."

And just like that, he seems to drift away.

I'm to blame for this, reader. You know it and I know it. Monty knows it and Carlo knows it. And Nancy knows it too. Whatever suffering Van went through today is on my head.

I listen carefully for the steady breathing that indicates Van is asleep. Strangely, it doesn't take long at all. Again, I blame myself for traumatizing him in such a way that sleep is his best escape.

I should leave right now, shouldn't I?

I should slip from this warm bed and from this comfortable apartment...and out of Van's life. He'd then be safe, as he deserves to be. Mayo and Jonah and Billy would have no reason to bother him again.

I lift my hand from his and slide an inch toward the edge of the bed. Only one inch, as this is just a test to check if Van's sleep is deep enough to make my getaway.

His hand snaps around my wrist.

Every muscle in my body grows rigid. "You're awake," I squeak. It's not a question, but it sounds like one.

"You promised to stay," Van replies, his tone dull. He rolls onto his side, away from me, to face the window.

"But it's all my fault."

"You didn't do anything to me. None of this is your fault." He pulls the silky purple puff up to his chin. All that's exposed of Van is a messy pile of multicolored hair. "But if you leave me now, George C, I will never forgive you."

My reaction to his statement is most surprising: instead of being conflicted, I'm intensely relieved. I don't want to go. I don't think I'm ever going to want to leave this man. And he just gave me the best reason in the world to stay put. "Then I'll stay."

I want to touch him. In my mind, I put my hand softly on his shoulder. I rub his back, and then I run my fingers through his hair. In reality, though, my hands stay at my sides. I close my eyes and wait for sleep to come.

*

We awaken to the ringing of Carol's cell phone on the floor in the leg pocket of my cargo pants. I climb out of bed and pull the phone from the deep pocket. I check the time before I answer it. It isn't morning yet—it isn't even midnight.

I don't recognize the number. "Hello?"

"George, it's Carol. Where are you? I've been worried sick."

Shit. "I'm so sorry I forgot to call you, Carol. I'm with Van, at his place." I glance at the bed. Van is buried in the blankets, still facing the wall. Somehow, I know he's awake.

"You found him? Is he all right?"

"Uh...I think so. I'll know more soon, I hope." I'm still in a zombie-like state from having been woken up from deep sleep by the ringing phone. "Where are you, Carol? And how are you calling me—I have your cell phone?"

"I'm at a neighbor's apartment in the building next door."

"God, I'm sorry I put you to so much trouble."

"I'm just glad to know you're okay and that you're with Van."

"Are you working tomorrow? I can stop by the store in the morning with your phone."

"Don't worry about my phone, dear. Just stop by the store when you have a few minutes so I can see with my very own eyes that you're all right."

"Okay. And sorry again about not contacting you."

"Hug Van for me, George, and be careful."

*

I slip back into the bed, and before I turn on my side to face him, I place the cell phone on the nightstand. "It was Carol," I tell him, as if he didn't hear my side of the conversation. "She was checking up on us."

His head moves. He's nodding.

"I figure Monty's gonna call pretty soon."

Van flips over to face me. "Why?"

I'm not as surprised as you'd expect that he's responding to me now. Van was in a trance of sorts, but he wasn't very far away from me at all. "He went to see Billy tonight. Your mom went with him."

"Jesus Christ." He sits up and crosses his legs. "I met that Billy-guy today. He's a bad person...dangerous, even. And my mother doesn't know when to shut up."

"Monty will keep your mom safe."

"I hope so."

I sit up beside him and lean against the headboard. "What happened to you today?"

"More of the same."

"What do you mean?"

"Just exactly what I said. Those guys dished out more of what Jake has been dishing out for years—threats and intimidation." Van's so cold, but he seems more angry than traumatized. "Billy's thugs grabbed me off the street before school. Tossed me in their truck. Terrorized me all day." He stops for a minute to brush his hair off his face. "Told me all the shit they were gonna do to me when we got back to Billy's house."

My heart sinks. Van knows how capable they are of hurting someone—he found me wheezing in the alley after they pummeled me. "They did it to get to me."

"I know. And I knew it when they were doing it. Too bad that little insight didn't stop me from freaking out."

I want to reach out to him. To pull him against me because he's started to shake. But I don't. I'm not sure if he wants me to.

"They brought me inside to meet Billy. He gave me a message for you, but I fucking refuse to be that asshole's message boy."

When I grab his shoulder, he flinches, and my heart sinks even lower in my chest. "What did he want you to tell me?"

"Weren't you listening to what I just said? I'm *not* that asshole's message boy."

I'm not sure if Van's trying to protect me from the message or if he's just being stubborn. "Did they hurt you?"

"Not physically. Mostly, I took verbal crap. Billy threatened to introduce me to a friend of yours—some guy named Mike."

"Fuck him."

"Is Mike the guy who raped you?"

"It wasn't rape. I let him do it."

"You call it what you want, and I'll call it what I want. Anyhow, is Mike the guy?"

"Yeah. He was the first of two guys. Then I was done with living that way."

Van shifts onto his knees beside me. "They're the worst kind of people. They probably sensed your vulnerability—and the sweetness in you—and took advantage of it. I don't blame you for what they made you do or for what they did to me."

"Those guys wouldn't know you were alive if it weren't for me."

"*I* wouldn't know I'm alive if it weren't for you either." He takes hold of my shoulders and gazes into my eyes. "You saved me from myself."

"But...but you were in a trance last night."

He doesn't look away. His eyes are now clear and blue—the hollowness is gone. "I was fucking terrified. Can you blame me?" Van gives me no chance to answer. "It took me a few hours to find myself again."

"You didn't even recognize me."

"I'd separated myself from the world. It's how I survived with Jake for so long, so it comes naturally when I'm scared. And I bet it's how you survived the nights with Mike and the other guy."

I remember wishing like hell I'd separate in two when Mike was fucking me. "I tried but I just couldn't do it."

"Then I have no clue how you got through it. Being able to leave my awareness behind saved my sanity."

I nod. "Well, it's over now, for both of us."

"And I'm here with you, so my fear is over too," he adds.

"I think we're gonna have to leave town though. You know, us two together."

He smiles. "We'll figure it out tomorrow."

I'm also willing to put the big decisions off until the morning. "Want to lie down and try to go back to sleep?"

"I want to lie down..." He pushes on my chest so I slide down into the sheets, and he lies close beside me.

"I was so scared I lost you, Van. I couldn't think straight."

Van's arm falls over my waist. "I know the feeling well. You also disappeared on me."

"How did you become part of me so...so effortlessly?" I don't really expect an answer.

"I wish I knew." Van's arm slides off my chest, and he climbs onto it. Blond hair falls into my face when he leans down to kiss me. His mouth is already open when it meets mine. The long, deep kiss stirs my desire for him.

"Let me make you feel good." I reach my hand into his boxers and squeeze his hardness. "I want to take you in my mouth."

He shakes his head.

"Why not?" His eyes are wide, gazing into mine without a hint of shyness, and his dick is ready for anything. "Why not?" I ask again.

"Because feeling good is gonna go both ways tonight, George C." He leans toward the night table and opens the drawer. "I've got a condom."

He hands it to me with a little tube. I get the picture. "You want to...are you saying you..."

Van places one finger over my lips to stop my rambling. "Just put it on."

I pull off my underwear, as does Van, and I roll on the condom. "I've never done this, you know, *to* somebody else."

"I know. It'll be a first for both of us." He rolls onto his belly, and I nudge him enough so he lets me place our pillow under his hips. I open the lube and squeeze some on my fingers. And then I get him ready for me.

Van moans as I prepare him. I can't stop myself from kissing his cheek, his neck, and his shoulders. He shudders, his head tilted back, his eyes half-closed. He's just so sexy. When my fingers sink into the place my dick will soon be, I can't help but moan along with him.

"I'm ready," he whispers after a few minutes of this amazingly intimate torture.

I want to stare into Van's eyes when I make love to him, so I try to turn him onto his back, but he resists. "I think it will be better if you stay behind me."

"Okay…" He's probably right, especially for our first time. I cover the condom with lube and climb onto him. I kneel between his legs and then push in and pull out—bit by bit, over and over again—until I've worked myself deep inside him. When he starts to pant, I hold still so he can adjust to me. As we lay together like a single person, I tell him the truth. "I love you, Van. And I always will, I can tell."

Van's breathing is noisier than ever before. Between quick breaths he says, "I didn't know…I'd be able to feel love…but I do. And I feel it for you, too."

Certain of his feelings for me, I'm instantly confident I can make love to him in a perfect way for us. We can love each other with our hearts *and* bodies. I begin to move; slow and shallow thrusts soon become deep and long. When it's too good to describe in mere words, I grit my teeth and hold back so I can be sure he's in heaven with me. I reach between his legs and find his hard dick pressed into the pillow and wrap my fingers around it. And I move my hand as I thrust.

People utter sappy things, I suppose, when they're about to experience pure release with the person they love. And we're no exceptions to this rule.

"Tell me we're forever, George C," Van utters as he comes into my hand.

"Forever won't be long enough," I say and let go inside him.

It may not be the most romantic thing to do, but I slide off Van and rush to the bathroom where I soak a clean hand towel in warm water. When I return, he's on his back and the pillow is on the floor beside the bed. Cleaning him turns into a moment I treasure, as it gives me a chance to study the lazy, satisfied smile I put on his face. Only after Van is clean and dry do I remove the condom and clean myself.

"We're gonna need a new pillowcase," he says, and his cheeks turn pink.

"I'm on it," I reply and grab one from his bureau's middle drawer. Carol's cell phone rings as I'm changing the pillowcase.

Van picks it up off the night table. He glances at me to be sure it's okay that he answers, and I nod. "Hello? Oh, hi Monty. Yeah, I'm okay. I'm with George C." He listens for a minute and then nods and says, "yeah" and "that's cool" a few times before he hangs up. The last thing he says is, "Thanks so much, Monty. I'll fill him in. And don't worry, I'll call my mother."

He pats the spot beside him on the bed. "Sit with me."

I drop the pillow on the bed and sit beside him. "That was Monty?"

"Uh-huh. He told me he made major progress with Billy. And then some..."

"How so?"

"He said he knows Billy from when they were much younger. Back then Billy worked for the guy who...who made Carlo do the same kind of shit you had to do. You know, what Billy made you do with Mike."

I can't think of a response. But I had no idea my life so closely mirrored Carlo's.

"Monty has some goods on Billy and his boss from way back. I guess they stole big money from some badass even worse than them, and Monty has proof of this. He actually used that information against Billy and his boss—to get them to release Carlo from prostitution about ten years ago. And he used the same threat to get Billy to call off his thugs now. They're gonna keep their distance from us."

"I usually don't believe in coincidences—and Monty just *happens* to have the goods on Billy?"

"Looks that way. But there's even better news. Monty told me he called a cop he's known forever at the Windsor PD. Told him all about what's been going on. Billy's not gonna get away with what he did to either of us. And neither are his thugs." Van's smile is kind of a wicked one; it gives me chills.

"So we can stay here?" I ask, trying to put it all together. It's hard to believe our problems are over.

"From what Monty says, we're off the hook for good. Billy, Jonah, and Mayo want nothing more to do with us, and when the cops get through with them, they're gonna wish they never messed with any of us." I don't think I've ever seen Van look so smug. "You have your job at the diner back, so they expect us both to be there tomorrow to work the brunch shift."

I fall back on the bed. I can't believe I'm free of the men who held so much over my head.

"We can both live here. We can work, do illustrations for Portals Literary Magazine, and start thinking about what we want to do in the future. Like maybe study art."

I'm honestly stunned. A few hours ago, I was a dude on the run who'd put the life of the guy he loves in jeopardy, and now I'm a dude with a lover and a home and a job and goals for the future. "Wow."

Van smiles at me. "It's kind of perfect, huh?" He steps out of the room and returns with his cell phone. "I told Monty I'd call Mom and let her know I'm okay."

He leaves one more time, and soon he's talking on his phone in the living room. I flip onto my belly and close my eyes, unable to believe that so much has changed in my life in such a short space of time. And positive changes, at last.

When Van returns, he says, "Well, it looks like we have a dinner invitation for tomorrow night after work. Mom seems serious about being part of our lives. *And* about putting some meat on our bones."

"I should probably stop by the thrift shop tomorrow before work and return Carol's phone. I also have to go to her place to pick up my stuff at some point."

"She's gonna be bummed to have you move out. Carol treats you like you are her own child."

"Then our next dinner date will have to be with Carol. We can take her out for Thai food to say thanks for everything," I decide. Van's right about how Carol looks at me with a mother's eyes.

"I think we've ended up with two mothers—Carol *and* Mom." Van seems kind of floored. Mostly in a good way.

"And two Dads—Monty and Carlo."

"You and I went from being orphans to having more parents than we can handle." He shakes his head. "But it's the middle of the night. We both had a rough day. Let's try to sleep."

We climb into our bed, and when he turns on his side to look out the window, I press my body along his entire length—his back against my chest, our legs intertwined. Yeah reader, like spoons. And we fit perfectly.

Part Five: Donovan

Saturday

WE GET UP early, take turns in the shower, eat peanut butter toast and drink coffee, and take a bus to the Second Chance Thrift Shop. I leave my top hat at home. I've been doing this a lot lately.

Carol is waiting for us.

"Boys, I'm going to need the details on what happened with your boss and that terrible man, Billy. But the store is busy today, so, as long as you're both safe, it can wait," she says after hugging each of us over the cash register.

She's right; the store is a madhouse this morning. It isn't the right time to talk. "We're safe now—Monty even got the cops involved—so no worries," George C assures her. "How about we take you out to dinner tomorrow night after work?"

"It'll be a thank you dinner for everything you've done." Carol really was the reason George C and I never lost touch when he was away, and she was the key to me finding him. Even if she hadn't intended to be.

She grins, pleased at the idea. "You boys can stop by my house whenever you have time today to pick up his stuff. I want you to keep the key; my home is always your home—and I'm talking to both of you."

"You're awesome, Carol."

"Before you go, I have a little gift for you both." She pulls a tall bag out from underneath the register. Inside are four rolled-up posters. "George told me how much you like superheroes, Van, and you had a hard time choosing which retro poster to buy. And so the rest of the retro superhero posters we have in stock are in this bag."

I've long considered my apartment a personal version of the Batcave. It's still a safe place, but maybe not so secret anymore. "Thanks so much. We'll hang them all over my apartment."

"Looks like we have a new superhero..." George adds. "Super Carol."

It's sappy—without a doubt—but we all smile because it's also kind of true.

"Well, then, I'll see you two right here after work tomorrow." We step aside, and Carol starts to help the next customer in line, but glances at him again and adds, "And, George...I like your sweatpants."

George C had to borrow my pink sweatpants and white T-shirt again, as his clothes are all at Carol's house. "I'm pretty in pink today."

He really is.

*

Carlo and Monty are waiting for us in the diner's break room before the brunch shift.

"Glad that you boys are together and happy," Monty says and winks. Maybe I cringe—it's not a crime. Thank God he didn't waggle his eyebrows. It may have pushed me over the edge.

"Thank you for helping us," George C replies. "We wouldn't be here together, in one piece, without you, sir."

Monty's chest puffs up a bit, and Carlo sniffs and then rubs his nose. "You boys have had some challenges, but hopefully, between Monty giving those thugs a good talking to and the information we provided to the police, it'll be smooth sailing from now on." He comes over to where we're standing in the doorway and gives us full-body hugs.

I have to grit my teeth to deal with all of this warm human emotion. Maybe I'm still not one hundred percent comfortable with group lovefests. In my defense, I've been a loner for years; it's going to take time for the scarecrow inside me to wither away and let my human part experience life. I hope I'll grow out of my discomfort with all things touchy-feely. So be patient with me, okay?

George C knows my limits, and he says, "It's time for us to get to work. Brunch waits for no one." He grabs my hand and pulls me toward the lockers.

I could kiss him.

Monty and Carlo look at each other and nod, and then George C and I pull on our aprons. I again forgo my lipstick, as I've been doing quite frequently lately, and pull my hair into a high ponytail. I'm ready to embrace the normal parts of my life, so I hurry onto the restaurant floor.

*

Between work and dinner with my mother, George C and I have a few hours to spend together—to celebrate our relationship and enjoy the freedom to walk around Windsor without fear of Billy and his thugs. Honestly, I'm not completely comfortable with either having a boyfriend or walking without fear—I don't think complete optimism is in my nature. But I *want* both of these things, and I'm willing to do everything I can to be a person, not a scarecrow.

And this means walking along the Lange River, hand in hand with the guy I love.

"Don't fight it, Vanny," George C says and squeezes my hand.

"When did you turn into a fucking mind reader?" I ask. You can't take all of the sarcasm out of the boy.

George C ignores my reply and pulls me down beside him onto a park bench. "Look." He points to a family flying a deep-blue kite on a still-grassy spot beside the river. I can easily spot the kite, but it blends in well with the crisp afternoon sky. I swear it's the same dad and two kids who were flying an orange kite the last time I sat on this very park bench—the morning George C left me.

Today is far less breezy than that day, and the kite, having achieved its optimum height, soars peacefully, high above the frigid water. And like last time, I identify with it. I'm no longer such an eyesore as when I related to the neon-orange kite set against a pale blue sky. Without the top hat and the unnaturally dark lipstick, people still see me, but they don't stop and stare and then glance away in discomfort and fear. "Hmmm...cold weather kite flying. Cool."

"Didn't Maria say we needed to come up with a family picture for the poem Mandy wrote about quality time?"

"Yeah, we do." I hand him my phone. "It takes great pictures."

George C grabs the phone and runs up to the father. He asks a question, and the man nods and smiles. Before he starts snapping photos, George C glances back at me, as if for reassurance, and it hits me he's still adjusting to this new life too. I give him a thumbs-up—yeah, it isn't a Van-like gesture, but whatever—and he goes to work.

I lean back and relax against the park bench. Even though it's cold outside, my shoulders aren't stiff and rigid. My jaw isn't clenched like a vise. My lips are bare. My worn top hat is in my closet at home. My black roots have faded to a dull gray. Am I still a scarecrow?

Maybe it doesn't matter what you call me, reader. And maybe instead of worrying about it, I'll keep on humming "Open Arms." The song's been stuck in my head since I bought George C the Journey album called *Escape*, even if we no longer need one.

*

Dinner with Mom is stiff and awkward, which is to be expected, right? We're not what you'd call a close family unit. And George C plays the very necessary role of glue. He somehow manages to keep the three of us stuck together for the hour it takes to eat our chicken potpies and drink glasses of ginger ale.

George C shovels in his final bite. "That was amazingly good. Thanks so much for inviting me to dinner, Nancy."

My mother's cheeks turn pink. "Well, thank you, George. I'm glad you liked it. The pies...well, I made them from scratch." She stares at me expectantly, as does George C.

Here's where I'm supposed to gush over my mommy's superior home cooking. "It wasn't half bad," I mutter. This is the best I can do under the circumstances. I've never been much of a yes-man. For good measure, I stuff the last forkful of chicken potpie into my mouth. It will prevent anything sarcastic from escaping my lips.

I barely have a chance to swallow when Mom moves to the edge of her seat. I can tell she has something on her mind and no plans to hold back on spilling it.

"I'm so glad you're both back here...or, uh, *back home*...safe and sound. And it appears as though the potential for danger is gone now." She slides back in the chair just slightly. "So, are you boys going to be living together now?"

"We're gonna be roommates," I say. It sounds less sappy than "living together." In my humble opinion.

"I'd like to offer to pay rent, Nancy," George C declares, focusing on Mom. It's like he read *her* mind this time.

"It would help out a lot...you know, since Jake moved out." My mother is practically drooling over George C and his kiss-ass behavior, but I'm glad. Harmony between my boyfriend and my mother simplifies my life. "We don't have to talk details tonight, though."

Good. I have more important things to do tonight.

*

It's still a challenge to let my guard down. I've had a wall of ice around me for so long. But it's getting easier, especially when I'm alone with George C. He melts the wall of ice into a puddle just by gazing at me with those earnest gray eyes. And keep this shit under your hat, reader: I crave alone time with him. I just can't get enough of it—his skin pressing against mine and the way I'm inhaling his breath. And other stuff... It warms me more than you'd ever believe.

I can hardly concentrate on Mom and her home-cooked dinner, as I was so needy for George C...on me. *In me.* I literally dragged him up the stairs before she had a chance to put a plate of cookies on the kitchen table. I'm in need of a different kind of dessert.

You're wondering who the hell I am now, aren't you? Because I'm certainly not the same asshole you met a few hundred pages ago. In fact, you actually turned back to the beginning of the book where I declared that no man would dazzle me into improved conduct and monogamy, just to check if I *really* made that claim. And another little thing I mentioned—that inspired sex, not to mention formulaic romance, would be among the missing in this dark tale of mine—well, it seems that I was wrong on that one too.

Here I am, lusting after the naked man who lounges before me on the silky purple bedspread, and not just because he's beautiful. And he *is* quite a magnificent sight, with chestnut brown curls falling over strong shoulders, and wide dark eyes looking eager and expectant. But I want him because he's the only person in the world I fully trust. When I'm with George C, I'm a real man—made of warm flesh and bone. Capable of feeling pain when bruised or broken, but equally capable of reaching the highest of highs. Even when we're apart, his presence in my life forces the scarecrow to keep its distance.

I pull off my boxers and stand before him at the end of the bed, hard and needy for him, and entirely unashamed of this. His eyes trace my body, head to toe and back, and settle on my eyes.

"You told me when we made love, it would wipe away the bad memories," George C utters.

"And?" I want to climb on top of him. To press my ear to his chest and listen to his heartbeat because it beats with love for me. But I don't—I wait. His answer is everything.

"And you were right. The memory is still part of me, but it doesn't haunt me like before."

I helped him get over his pain. The knowledge propels me forward onto the bed, where I kneel above him and study his eyes. "I want you so much, George C."

He gazes up at me, surprised by my candor. "Van..."

To be honest, I'm shocked that I revealed this bare truth, as well, but I don't let it inhibit me. I have an agenda here. I need this man, and I'm going to help myself to what he's offering. I lower my body to his and press my lips into the hollow of his neck. He shivers and it feeds my passion. Before my lips find his, I explore the sensitive spot behind his ear and the entire length of his throat with my mouth and tongue. When I shift my focus to his jaw and then his temple, George C groans and presses his dick against my leg. But I don't thrust against him. Not yet.

Instead, I lavish attention on the other side of his face. I plan to leave no part of his handsome face needy for attention.

"Please, Van...kiss me."

I pull off George C enough to peer into his eyes. They're open, waiting for this visual connection with me. "So much has changed," I whisper, and it once again hits me how much I feel for him. I touch our lips together.

George C opens his mouth in invitation, but I resist.

"We'll kiss when you're inside me." I reach to the bedside table, yank open the drawer, and pull out the things we need. "I'll get us ready."

He nods just once as he's in a lust-filled daze, which I find perfectly adorable. I have to fight with myself not to kiss him because I'm so hungry for his lips. But I'm *starving* for the whole package. So I cover my fingers with lube and reach back and prep my ass for his invasion. George C stares at me with glazed-over eyes, as if I'm an enthralling YouTube video. As he watches, he licks his lips and grips my knees with clenched fists. When I roll the condom onto his dick, he closes his eyes and wrinkles his forehead. He's probably doing a mind control exercise because he's worried he'll come too soon. But I don't care, as long as he's in me when he comes, and our lips are pressed together.

I lift myself above him and gradually lower my ass onto his dick. It's slow going as I'm tight as hell. I'm not going to lie; I'm stretched to my limit well before I've met my goal. But when George C is finally all the way inside, his eyes still closed and his forehead wrinkled in concentration, I lean forward and cover his lips with my open mouth. His tongue darts out and tangles with mine, and we sigh. It's like coming home.

This time I do all the work, so the kiss can't last for long. I sit up, and then lift and lower myself again and again as he strokes my dick. Our eyes are now open, and we take each other in. George C in heaven, one I have provided with my body, is a sight I refuse to miss. And when he stiffens, I lean down and press my lips to his and keep them there until both of us come.

What happens next...words of love, yes, and the way we study each other... Look away, reader, just for a few seconds. I willingly invited you to join me in our story, but I need to share this moment with George C alone.

You'll be sorry if you miss my clever postscript

IT'S JUNE. YEAH, time flies when you're having a fucking blast. Which, I realize, sounds sarcastic, but remember, reader: I don't lie. Uh-huh, I'm totally for real when I tell you that the rest of my senior year was about as good as it gets. At least, so far in *my* life.

George C and I shared Thanksgiving and Christmas with Mom and Carol. All four of us together at my house for both holidays. The food was fucking amazing. As in, total food comas for George C and me. And I can't get enough of those touching family moments. (Yes, *that* was sarcastic.)

FYI: I was George C's Valentine, and I mean this in an official sense. He got down on one knee on our rainbow rug, right beside the coffee table—with a rose between his teeth—and asked, "Will you do me the great honor of being my Valentine, Vanny?" Maybe the question came out sounding sort of garbled—thanks to the thorny stem poking into his lips—but I knew what he wanted and agreed to it. To prevent additional bloodshed.

We skipped the Windsor Academy senior prom because neither of us knows how to dance, and we like eighties ballads, not pop and rap. But we went to an after party at Tad's house, or maybe *mansion* is a better word for the huge compound Tad calls home. It was basically the soccer team and their dates and the staff of Portals Literary Magazine at the party. A strange blend of people, I know, but now that I'm no longer a scarecrow-loner, an occasional social event happens every now and then. I'm fine with this, especially since none of the other kids seem to be particularly scared of me anymore. It's almost like I fit in.

In May, I hung a finished copy of *Portals Literary Magazine*—which we dedicated to the staff's devoted friend, George C—on the big bulletin board in the break room at the Monty-Carlo Diner. George C cried when he opened it and saw his name.

And slowly but surely, justice is coming for Billy. Several times each, George C and I have sat down with the cops for drawn-out and detailed Q and A sessions. Not exactly a stroll in the park. But from what I hear, Billy's off the streets as he waits for what comes next. A guilty plea, or a trial maybe. Monty tells us that important shit takes time.

Newsflash: I buzzed off my straw-like hair two days before graduation. Kept it bleached blond though. I look more like a Q-tip than a scarecrow these days, which is probably a good thing. George C loves to run his hand over my head. He says it feels like velvet. I'm cool with this too.

I still wear way too much plaid flannel and denim, but I'm saving my money for art school so new clothes aren't my top priority. George C is saving up his cash, too. We're not going to start school this fall, though. Right now, we're satisfied with life just the way it is. Nope, you don't need to get your hearing checked, bookworm. You heard me right—full-time hours at the Monty-Carlo Diner, hanging out with kids from school and work, and spending quality and quantity family time with Carol and Mom keep us pretty busy, and we're happy. We plan for art school and share graphic novels every night on the couch. Life is pretty damned good.

If you're still reading at this point, maybe it's because you relate to me in some small way. Well, reader, I'm not going to reach out of the book and pat you on the head, or anything, but I will say this: Leave *your* scarecrow days behind. You won't miss them at all.

About the Author

Mia Kerick is the mother of four exceptional children—one in law school, another a professional dancer, a third studying at Mia's alma mater, Boston College, and her lone son finally off to college. (Yes, the nest is empty.) She has published more than twenty books of LGBTQ romance when not editing National Honor Society essays, offering opinions on college and law school applications, helping to create dance bios, and reviewing scholarship essays. Her husband of twenty-five years has been told by many that he has the patience of Job, but don't ask Mia about this, as it's a sensitive subject.

Mia focuses her stories on the emotional growth of troubled people in complex relationships. She has a great affinity for the tortured hero in literature, and as a teen, Mia filled spiral-bound notebooks with tales of tortured heroes and stuffed them under her mattress for safekeeping. She is thankful to NineStar Press for providing her with an alternate place to stash her stories.

Her books have been featured in Kirkus Reviews magazine and have won an Ippy Gold Award for YA fiction, a Rainbow Awards for Best Transgender Contemporary Romance and Best YA Lesbian Fiction, a Reader Views' Book by Book Publicity Literary Award, the Jack Eadon Award for Best Book in Contemporary Drama, an Indie Fab Award, a Royal Dragonfly Award for Cultural Diversity, and a Story Monsters Purple Dragonfly Award for YA Fiction, among other awards.

Mia Kerick is a social liberal and cheers for each and every victory made in the name of human rights. Her only major regret: never having taken typing or computer class in school, destining her to a life consumed with two-fingered pecking and constant prayer to the Gods of Technology. Contact Mia at miakerick@gmail.com or visit at www.miakerickya.com to see what is going on in Mia's world.

Facebook: www.facebook.com/mia.kerick

Twitter: @MiaKerick

Instagram: www.instgram.com/Mia_Kerick_author

Other books by this author

Love Spell

The Art of Hero Worship

Scarred

Also Available from NineStar Press

Connect with NineStar Press

www.ninestarpress.com

www.facebook.com/ninestarpress

www.facebook.com/groups/NineStarNiche

www.twitter.com/ninestarpress

www.tumblr.com/blog/ninestarpress